# *IN CELEBRATION OF ALL THAT BURDENS US*

Poems

Essays

Stories ...

**Ségun Ògúntólá**

Seaburn Publishing Group
P. O. Box 2085
Astoria N.Y. 11102
www.seaburn.com



Edited by Glenn Statile, Ph.D.

ISBN 1-59232-084-8

Printed in the United States of America

"Ben Okri: A Rousing Bard" appeared earlier, in slightly different form, in *the African* (July 2001) as "A Griot Whose Resonating Voice Rouses Consciousness"; "The Time Traveler" appeared earlier, in slightly different form, in *the African* (October 2001); "The Thoughts of a Man Who Recently Reunited with His Destiny" originally appeared at *nigeriansinamerica.com*; "My Mother Whimpering on the Bed of History" originally appeared in different form as "Inside the Thoughts of a Woman Raped by History" in *QBR the Black Book Review*, Vol. 9, No. 4, July-August 2002.

To
Irene Schneider and Karen Campbell
(for, in particular, November 2004)

And to
Stephanie Wickersham, and Nya Joy
(God speed; we will meet again)

## Author's Note

Literature yearns to sing to us anew about Existence, about our tumultuous age, our unsettling personal and societal concerns; soothes our aches, celebrates our life in all its manifold complexities, counsels and gives us hope. Wise, Literature: it aims to do so by creating a tranquil psychical space for us in thoughtful books, in which, in solitude, it can engross us in thought about Existence, impart knowledge. I strive to be a conduit for Literature in its noble endeavor.

*My mind like fire, searching*

Jessica Williams

## CONTENTS

### PART ONE

### POEMS



### PART TWO

**ESSAYS**



**STORIES**

# POEMS
# PART ONE

## The Broken Hearted

Your body you offer
readily
a sacrifice to carnal pleasure.

Your heart you guard
fiercely
a weighty nugget of pure gold
your lifeline.

I wonder who had hurt you so
my dear.

Claw your anguish onto my face
beat your wild rage onto my chest
wet my neck with your salty sorrow
let my tranquility be a haven for your troubled spirit.

Me
your august scapegoat
noble offering to
absolve you
of this perennial grief
plaguing you so.

**My Restless Nymph**

Hugs
kisses on cheeks
gentle caresses of shoulder blades and
laughter round the table where bottles of wine
sat breathing.

Everyone is now gone
the world is asleep.

I lay on my bed thinking of you
ogling your picture
gazing at your blue star eyes
your fine crescent moon lips
recalling
how your nose twitches when you blush
our enlightening discussions of ideas
lamenting
you are not here with me
wondering
why you
my dear restless nymph
chose this night
the night of my arrival in this world
to abandon me.

## Beloved

I recently happened upon a letter you once wrote me.
You will be coming home this weekend, you wrote,
and wish you could just come over to surprise me
but you knew it was not a good idea.
You are so proud of me
happy to hear from me
happy to hear that
I am nearing the end of my debut novel.
You do miss me
you were thinking the other day
of the first week we started dating and
you came over on a Sunday
ate, then went right to bed and
I watched you sleep.
"Anyway, let me not be too mushy," you ended the letter.
That was over four year ago when,
lacking the will to disobey the Word,
Thou Shall Not Be Unequally Yoked,
you gave up on us.
You are now married to
one equally yoked and
about to have your first child.
I am at my desk
making the final edits to
the novel
no publisher yet.

## Angelic You

The way to a woman's heart is
not by the man begging on his knees.
I wish it were
I would have,
when I was out with you last night,
held your hands
gazed into your eyes
begged you to be mine
the hot New York City sidewalk
scorching my knees through the
thin fabric of my trousers
curious passersby looking on
subtle smile animating their faces.

You
golden hearted you
steadfastly dedicated to the wellbeing of your Family
You
sylph you
your lustrous skin the color of sunset
bright eyes full of energy
like a star
sculptural lips
like quarter moons.
You
witty you
your imagination vast and wondrous
like the Universe.
You
angelic you
who found me hurt
soothed my pain
calmed my agitated heart
captured my imagination
one day on the train
a chance encounter ended too soon when

I had to disembark soon afterward
cursing my fate in life
as I stood on the platform watching that
bastard hastily steal you away from me
clutching my only consolation;
my only hope of seeing you again
the piece of paper I had hastily torn from
a magazine I had with me and
on which you had scribbled your e-address.

I thought of you often since that day
wondered why you never responded to my mail
often gazed at the paper bearing your address
which I had glued onto the door of my refrigerator.

Little did I know then that
twenty four moons hence
you would contact me.
Intense, my joy when
I heard from you and
happier still when you readily accepted my
invitation to dinner.

Here I am now back home alone
giddy from the bliss of our dinner rendezvous
wondering what would become of our renaissance
Friendship?
Romance?

**A Queen and Her Crown**
(for Mika, a Desire)

When they met
she instantly recognized him.
Staring into his eyes
she tenderly held his hand.
The emotional cross in him
immediately lost its, often,
depressing gravity.
"What took you so long, my queen?" he said.
"I am here now, my bejeweled crown," she said,
still staring into his eyes,
her noble face graced by a hearty smile.

## Blues for Ségun

I
He has a communal heart
an endangered species in
a world plagued with individualism.

Dejected at finding no committed support in
our increasingly atomized, self-seeking family he
resolved to stay alone
writing, steadfastly
transforming his grief, joy, hope into
literature.

II
Not finding committed support among men he
thought of turning to the gods and
realized he would thereby sell his soul to the Devil.

III
And so it was that
one day he disappeared back
into the belly of his mother
bobbed about her womb
up to her neck
her throat
her chin
her forehead
her scalp
and eventually nestled comfortably in
the back of her skull.

## A Vulnerable Moment

Running on danger level
should refuel

There is a station here, somewhere
Don't know exactly where
cannot find it
but I know it is here, somewhere
Will I find it?

## A Lone Wolf

The day of the lone wolf is over.
We should gather ourselves
and proceed as One.

Heavy on my heart
this realization
for they have not comprehended this
nor have the will.

Here I am
cloistered in the
paradise of Literature
awaiting an enlightened pack.

## Caveat for Men Seeking Knowledge I

All ye men seeking Knowledge
beware of the wrath of the gods
and, worse, the
ridicule of your fellow men.

Like the gods
master the art and science of cunningness,
be prudent and cryptic in your utterances, your letters.

## Caveat for Men Seeking Knowledge II

(Or Ode to Social Dementia)

I woke up one morning and
realized that
I could no longer exist in
the world as a
"normal" human being.

Now over
my dapper days, my days of salmon and wine and roses
here I am existing on
the margin of society
my shelter the streets, the trains
my food meager and dependent on
the caprice of passersby
my clothing shabby
my star eyes betraying my
luminous mind
a subtle smile animating my
serene face.

Beware
the psychological and emotional
consequence of
attaining Knowledge.

**A Prayer for S**

She was vivacious
bright the light in her eyes.
I liked her immediately
warmed up to her
mustered the strength to ignore her
fierce-looking greyhound
glowering at me.
Our mutual friend, her
fellow graduate student
in Washington DC,
had taken me to meet her
in Virginia where
she then lived
with her boyfriend,
later husband.

The second time I met her
"You smell good," she said
as we embraced.
Her kind remark warmed my heart
causing a gentle smile to
animate my face.
We were in Portland where
our mutual friend had moved from
New York City
to honor our mutual friend's husband whose
paintings were being acknowledged with
a solo exhibition.
I had journeyed there from
New York City
she and her husband from nearby
San Francisco
Where they had moved from
Virginia.
As our mutual friend drove us from
the airport to her charming farmhouse,

"The Flying Pig",
we chatted
discussed ideas.
Later that day we all sat
round the dining table
indulging in our passion for
discussing ideas
the fireplace glowing
the aroma of freshly brewed coffee
and bouquet of wine
scenting the air.
We talked about her course load and students
we talked about the state of the world
we agreed the world needs
Love
Tolerance
Cross-cultural understanding.
Such was how we spent those glorious days.
I have not seen her since.

Not long ago
our mutual friend told me this
on the telephone:
"You would not recognize her.
She got quite thin.
The treatment has been hard on her.
Please pray for her."
I imagined her bald
gone her bountiful hair.

I recently spoke with her
on the telephone.
She was in Portland with her husband
visiting our mutual friend
a Thanksgiving Day rendezvous
I was unable to attend.
"I appreciate your courage,
your will to life.

Remain strong," I said.
"Thank you," she said.
She was cheerful
I felt her soft smile
her strength
her love of Knowledge
her love of Life
her will to live.
As I hung up the telephone,
"May she live!"
I said out loud,
gazing at the heavens.

## I Wonder If She Still Loves to Dance

In New York City, a glorious temple
dedicated to the glory of Music.
There, diligent disciples pay homage
singing various songs
in diverse tongues.

Not long ago
from the temple
a song dear to my heart.
I sat swaying to the song
my rocking chair creaking
a bottle of wine heightening my senses
my head at rest on some volumes in my bookshelf
tears soon waltzing down my cheeks, salting my lips,
sweet the pain of remembrance.

Nya Joy was her name
it was with her I last heard the song
souls in trance, us two
blissfully riding on the ethereal wings of Music.

Now that she resides in the netherworld,
this Joy of a Nya,
I wonder if she still loves to dance.

**Sweden 2004**
(for Isaach Ḍe Bankolé)

Now that you have survived the inferno
and are about to depart
to conquer the first of your crosses
in this phase of your being here,
I say to you:
Go,
fulfill your destiny
make proud the girls, her, me, the blood.
That's our pa, the girls would say, giggling.
That's my man, she would say, smiling.
That's my loyal blood, I would say, moist-eyed.
He is the one, the blood would, at last, acknowledge.

Though we love you,
To Her only you belong.

I bid you farewell
entrust you to the guidance of them who
have come and gone before you
whose footsteps you are fated to follow in
devotion to Her.

**Dusza**
(for Krzysztof Kieslowski)

Having presented Men the
last of his great testament,
he was ready for Home
his work Here done.

His star eyes ablaze,
he had started seeing images, scenes
Divine
Timeless
Spaceless
Eternal beauty.

No wonder when asked what he's going to do next
"Sit in a room and smoke," he said.
What he didn't tell the interviewer:
He was going to sit in a room, smoking, awaiting
the Chariot then coursing through the heavens enveloped
in a cloud of colors, yellow, blue, green, coming
to carry him Home in fanfare
organ clanking, Trumpets blaring.

**23305**

Who knew Knowledge,
like Love,
could be so devastating.

Now ended
my decade long sojourn in the netherworld,
I reemerge in this world with sharp eyes, humbled;
my bygone blurred vision of the world
a reminder of the fated ignorance of even the most educated of men.
Knowledge is not earned but a gift of the Dead, of the gods.
Blessed and cursed both
the man on whom It is bestowed.

Though today I begin my four hundred and sixty nine moons in life,
having died and recently reborn in knowledge
I am in fact a new born child,
dependent on the caprice of the gods,
the lords of this world,
for my survival.

I begin my life anew,
with certain trepidation,
for I will in cipher speak to men
of the secret of the gods
and like those before me
will suffer the consequence.

## A Plea

I have gotten you working overtime
for a long time now.
Of this I know you are not happy,
as you more and more make known to me daily
in pronounced visceral messages.

I am not by nature abusive, I assure you.
I must give you respite, I know.
I often, in fact, think of doing so,
but this daily rendezvous of mine with Bliss, you see,
I need more and more
to sing of the anguish of man.

So, my dear lifeline,
bear with me a while longer
as I hasten to fulfill my destiny
and then lay us down to sleep.

# POEMS
# PART TWO

**The Age-old Conundrum**

The boundary has been set.
Here are the rules
the particulars of the Law:
. . .
Any questions?
. . .
None?
. . .
Very well.
Let the game of History begin.
(Would be) historians, heed
the drama of Existence.

**Africa's Tears and Laughter**

The Shadow of the Sun
Something Out There

Things Fall Apart
Two Thousand Seasons
An African Elegy
Astonishing the Gods

Modern Africa
The Open Sore of A Continent
The Black Man's Burden
Let Freedom Come: Africa in Modern History

## Nothing Comes from Violence

Nothing comes from violence
nothing ever could
so men say
their illusion.

The gods know,
obviously,
the reality of being
the reality of this world:
Everything comes from violence
Everything.

## A Tapestry of Hope Woven of Music

Immigrant Slave Song
Africa Tears and Laughter

North and South
Gods and Men
Why Can't We Live Together

Opposite People
Confusion
Dog Eat Dog
Sorrow Tears and Blood
Underground System
Army Arrangement
No Agreement

Uprising
Buffalo Soldiers
Bustin' Out Of Trenchtown
The Trance Of Seven Colors

Filles De Killimanjaro
See-Line Woman
Tar Baby
Sankofa
New Moon Daughter
Four Women
Black, Brown, & Beige
Multikulti
Strange Fruit
Naima
Cousin Mary
India
Mr. P.C.
Get Up Stand Up
Let It All Out
Thulasizwe / I Shall Be Released!

Lively Up Yourself
Rejoice
Message From Home
Our Roots Began In Africa
Heaven's Here On Earth

Exodus
Traveling Miles
Miles Ahead
Kind of Blue
Walkin'
In A Silent Way

The Jungle Line
The Hissing of Summer Lawns
Electric Africa
Money Jungle

Crossroads
New Beginning

Live-Evil
Bitches Brew
You're Under Arrest

Terrestrial Beings
One Love People /
Get Ready

Gondwana
Pangaea
Renaissance
It's About That Time

Miles Smiles

## On a Night Journey, a Scene Witnessed, Chorus Heard

(for the slaves of History)

Our brother
having been to the mountain top
seen the promised land
assured us we will get there.

Some in the family,
the doubting Thomases,
did not believe our brother
failed to comprehend that
he was
the god of love
the lamb of History
sacrificed on
the Altar of History
so that we might
one day be
*truly* free.
At last!
here we are
on our way
to the promised land
our feet blistered by
the thorny plantation of History
our bodies fatigued from
toiling in Its fields, Its industries
our spirit light
Joy in our hearts
Music on our lips
plenty red wine
baguette
blue cheese and
moist aromatic tobacco
in our sacks.

# ESSAYS

## Ben Okri: A Rousing Bard

> Those who have lived with nature, those who have suffered the erosion of unexplored paths of history, cannot afford to be silent, to be cowardly, and to think only of themselves.
>
> -Ben Okri, "Among the Silent Stones"

In his acclaimed book, *The Soccer War*, in the chapter titled "Lumumba", Ryszard Kapuscinski, the famed Polish journalist, writes this about Africa:

> "[. . . ] The awakened Africa [he is here referring to the continent in the late 1950s / early 60s, the time many of its countries achieved "independence"] needs great names. As symbols, as cements, as compensations. For centuries the history of the continent has been anonymous. In the course of 300 years traders shipped millions of slaves out of here. Who can name even one of the victims? For centuries they fought the white invasions. Who can name one of the warriors? Whose names recall the suffering of the black generations, whose names speak of the bravery of exterminated tribes? Asia had Confucius and Buddha, Europe Shakespeare and Napoleon. No name that the world would know emerges from the African past. More: no name that Africa itself would know. (First Vintage International Edition, New York, P. 49)

It is impossible for any thoughtful one of us to read that passage and not squirm in discomfort. For if asked to name world-historical personages from the African past, the majority of us would scratch their heads, stroke their beards, their moustaches; run their palms over their braids, tug at their locks, their ponytails; avert their eyes, stare into space. (Myself included, of course, except I would be biting the tip of my middlefinger, a habit that betrays any one or all of these: I am musing on a question or an idea; I am lamenting my ignorance of an issue I ought to have known about; or I am steadying my quivering lips and chattering teeth in order to stifle the spurt of emotion then welling up in my heart, moistening my eyes with tears so eager to wiggle down my cheekbones, snake down my cheeks and onto my lips, the salty water stinging my wounded emotion, heightening my sense of grief, making me lose the battle, and thus defeated, release my middlefinger from the sharp clutches of my incisors and begin to sob shamelessly, as I once did at The Film Forum, in New York City, while watching Ousmane Sembene's poignant film, "Ceddo.")

How could we name world-historical personages from the African past? (I suspect that except for hastily mentioning Shaka Zulu, say, thanks to the famous biographical movie about his life and times, the majority of us would indeed be unable to name any world-historical personages from Africa's past.) Our ancestors were customarily oral. And our spiritual-others (gods), pantheons and cultural artifacts with which we would have been able to readily reconstruct our glorious past were plundered. And cunningly exploiting the social malady that is war among peoples, they plotted and nurtured the trade in flesh, shipped their human purchases, their investment, to the inferno of plantations across the seas. And it did not stop there, for to totally kill a tree (society / culture), you uproot it. Accordingly, this became the fate of those of us who were not purchased, left on the continent to suffer the spiritual and bodily agonies of colonialism:

Our indigenous shrines were forcibly replaced by mosques and churches; our indigenous judicial systems were forcibly replaced by the court of Sharia law, the court of modern "rational law."

Our indigenous way of life undermined, defeated, we became demoralized; everything fell apart! And our brothers and sisters shipped across the sea, in the Diaspora, were diligently bred and bled to commerce's content, to the bank: the investor must reap the profit of his strong, resourceful, human-machine.

Those who altered our (Africa's) destiny—re-wrote our history, stole millions of our people and shipped them to strange lands across the Atlantic where they bled them for material gain, the development of their society; colonized the rest of our people left on the continent; exploited (and continue to exploit) our mineral, natural and human resources for the development of their society; lied to the modern world that our people had nothing worthy of praise in our history, that we were merely "barbarians," and thus denied the world the knowledge of Africa's ancient civilization, thereby causing and sustaining ignorance and bigotry that is plaguing the world today, undermining cross-cultural understanding and tolerance . . . those who did these things took meticulous, demonic measures to ensure that we do not recall the names of our ancestors, our ancient warriors, our ancient heroes and heroines. So, it is not shocking that we are today unable to readily identify an African Confucius, Buddha or Shakespeare. We need not include Napoleon: we know he was a white Shaka, as Miriam Makeba ingeniously pointed out in the song, "U Shaka", responding to the notion that Shaka was an African Napoleon.

Our ignorance of our African past, of our unsung world-historical personages, ancient warriors, ancient heroes and heroines, artists, thinkers, historians, astronomers, healers, engineers . . . because of historical forces beyond our control is forgivable. What cannot be forgiven—-for it undermines our knowledge of ourselves, our history and heritage, failures and triumphs, our happiness—-is our ignorance of them today.

Many of us today, perhaps, know of some of our noteworthy modern personages and of their works. But how many of us know of Ben Okri, that child of Africa rightly recognized as one of the greatest writers alive today? How many of us are familiar with his literary universe, that wondrous world of Thought luminous with dazzling intellect, energized with passion for the freedom and wellbeing of our peoples, of all peoples; a wondrous world of Thought where Wisdom—-manifest in printed words; manifest in visual and animate prose—gazes, smiles at the reader?

We too often are ignorant of and, therefore, do not

appreciate our flagbearers, our warriors who today are resolutely—sometimes at the expense of their wellbeing—-bearing our historical and racial cross, struggling for our freedom. I am often reminded of this bitter truth; this ignorance of the majority of us, each time I ask one of us if she or he is familiar with the name Okri, reads his work. The body language and verbal response are always the same: a narrowing of the eyes, and, eventually, a "No . . . I don't know him." To that question someone once responded: "Isn't he a musician." "No," I said, disappointed. "He is a writer, one of the most luminous stars in the universe of literature today. You know, it is a shame that we too often do not know our cultural warriors," I, impassioned, said. "You have a way with words. You really are a writer," he said, smiling. The conversation ended in a joke of some sort, whereupon, red wine breathing in our goblets, we jabber: "So, what's going on?" "Nothing much. Working, writing." "Me too, my brother. Gotta pay those darn monthly bills."

For lack of vision my people perish, says the adage. Inspired, Sadé Adú tells us on her "Slave Song":

> [...]
> Teach my beloved children
> who have been enslaved
> to reach for the light continually
>
> Wisdom is the flame
> Wisdom is the brave warrior
> who will carry us into the sun
> [...]

The relationship between wisdom and vision: the former is indispensable to the latter; the latter is truly what frees a person or people from existential bondage, makes it possible to dream an idea (latent reality) and realize it (transform it into an overt, empirical, reality). I think of the trajectory like this: social consciousness→knowledge→wisdom→vision. How to rouse social consciousness? One way is to read Literature, voraciously. (Note that I said Literature and not books: there is a huge difference between both. Literature profoundly explores existence; books are expressly concerned with (usually written for) social engineering, for entertainment, for "Self Help." Whereas Literature might do these, it does so intrinsically; they are not its express purpose. Ralph Ellison's *Invisible Man*, say, and Ben Okri's *A Way of Being Free* are literature. Examples of books abound, the reader will recall some of them.)

Okri is one of those extant writers who aim to and do rouse social consciousness, impart knowledge; one of those writers whose work is of cosmic proportion. He is famous in Europe, especially in Great Britain, but less known here in the United States. And I suspect we do not constitute the majority of those who read his work here.

In a poignant moment of reflection (or was it a revelation?), Omovo, the main character in Okri's novel, *Dangerous Love*, says:

> [. . .] - and I am here on these shores, in this strange town, weighted down by soul-clog of useless knowledge, of other people's opinions, the creative dangers of thinking in an imposed language – betrayed by language – erased from history – deceived – as children, we read how the whites discovered us – didn't we exist till they discovered us? - weighted down by manipulated history, rigged history books, rigged maps of the continent – weighted down by lies – and then believing those lies – swallowing them – force-feeding ourselves with them – gorging ourselves –
> [. . .] transfiguration – transfigure the deception multiplied by education – all education is bad until you educate yourself – from scratch – start from the beginning, from the simplest things – assume nothing – question everything – begin again the journey from the legends of creation – look again at everything – keep looking – be vigilant – understand things slowly – digest thoroughly – act swiftly – re-dream the world – restructure self – all the building blocks are there in the chaos – USE EVERYTHING – USE EVERYTHING

WISELY – EVERYTHING HAS SIGNIFICANCE – ” (Hardcover Edition, ps. 294-295)

Surely, Omovo’s thoughts speak to us: we and he are one; we and he are inhabitants of the same psychic universe, our life bound by the same agonizing social reality, that reality born of our plague of a historical experience, Africa’s contact with the world outside of her.

In that paragraph, Okri, through Omovo, aims to rouse our social consciousness.

To read Okri’s work is to take flight into a wondrous realm of Thought: a realm where the reader is sure to meet Wisdom, and, consequently, begins to realize that the human world is one of endless possibilities, that the capacity for endless possibilities is the one and only true human nature; a realm where the reader begins to realize that Universal Love (Freedom) is and must be the ultimate goal of human existence; a realm where one will hear the insistent echo of the divine, visceral cry that cross cultural understanding must be truly realized in this world. Any wonder this was written: ‘Okri’s writing is hailed for its intelligence, tenderness, poeticism and luminosity … Okri is an important writer because of the startling clarity and determination of his humanism’ (Financial Times).

Accolades of this sort ought to make us proud of Okri. For he is one of the modern bards Africa sent to the world to hauntingly wail her story, and that of her denied children, many of whom are today scattered all over the world looking for the sun; to hauntingly wail of her struggle, since her house was felled, for adequate food, clothing and shelter; to hauntingly wail of her struggle to dance again, smile again, laugh again; to hauntingly wail and keep wailing for her true liberation, both from within and from without; to keep wailing until his central message is heeded: Universal Love is the destiny of the human family and must be realized in this world.

Although the wellbeing of Africa, of all her children is a great concern of Okri, it would be a grave mistake to assume his work is (or deem it) limited to exploring African issues. In its totality his work concerns the wellbeing of the entire human family. Consequently, his work is thoughtfully universal: the cerebral emancipation—-through the potent, transforming power of Thought—-of humanity from the jungle existence it is in today; the realization of Universal Love in the human world, for the human family is One, its members sharing one home, planet Earth, their destinies intertwined. This essentially means we have no choice but to truly love and care for one another, regardless of race or creed.

The trans-African, universal dimension of Okri's work is most evident in his reflective volume of essays, *A Way of Being Free*. (If one reads only one work by Okri, this volume, I think, ought to be it. And one ought to read it at least twice, the most rewarding way to read.) And also his story of Azaro—the spirit-child experiencing an earthly existence—narrated in a trio of novels: *The Famished Road*, *Songs of Enchantment* and *Infinite Riches*. The universality of Azaro's story explains why those novels have been called "world-vision or world-book" (Scotsman). About *The Famished Road*, Robert Yates of *Time Out* wrote: 'This is a book to generate apostles. People will be moved and, stars in their eyes, will pass on the word.' Linda Grant of Independent on Sunday wrote: 'Reading Okri felt to me like talking to someone who has a secret.' Harry Eyres of The Times thought the book: 'One of the truly great post-war novels.' About his discerning, knowledge-imparting novel, *Astonishing the Gods*, these responses have been written: 'In this powerful, sensuous and philosophical book, I saw universal aspects of the human condition like loneliness, joy, survival, despair, courage, oblivion, pain, terror, optimism and knowledge … Okri's use of language is beautifully, thrillingly and vibrantly poetic. Smiles can be heard; silences have melodies; sounds have colours and tenderness has a fragrance … You will probably be as enchanted, intellectually challenged and moved (almost to tears) as I was.' (*European*) 'Ben Okri is a writer for whom to be grateful. He embodies a questing spirit and a questioning disposition … such a writer is rare, an endangered species.' (*Scotland on Sunday*) 'Astonishing the Gods is properly worked and exact, and fulfils Calvino's prescription for lightness – being like a bird, rather than a feather … This novel is like a forbiddingly high-sided mountainous pass ... Reaching it is a rare achievement ... This is an impressive, brave and often beautiful book.' (*New Statesman & Society*) And, about Okri's impassioned epic verse for the wellbeing of humankind in the twenty-first century, *Mental Fight* ("An Anti-Spell for the 21st Century"), this has been written: 'An angry, hopeful, weary, wary, epic reveille to the human spirit.' (*The Times*)

This rare recognition of Okri, the honors that have been bestowed on him and the esteemed literary prizes his work has won are well deserved. For Okri is brilliantly illuminating the path to Knowledge. All who care to follow and persevere will meet Knowledge, have everlasting life in cross-cultural understanding.

Ben Okri, our gem. Well deserving of our knowledge and recognition. We ought to celebrate him, write him into (our) history for being yet another African pioneer who triumphed against daunting hardship to tell our story, the human story, so that the world might come to know, truly.

"Wisdom is the flame / Wisdom is the brave warrior / who will carry us into the sun. Ignorance and apathy undermines knowledge, begets and fosters cerebral and spiritual poverty. Without knowledge, there is no wisdom; without wisdom, there is no vision; without vision, there is no true emancipation and progress. For lack of vision my people perish. Let us continually seek and support our vision bearer. And take to heart the message implicit in this first stanza of Okri's poem, "An African Elegy":

> We are the miracles that God made
> To taste the bitter fruit of Time.
> We are precious.
> And one day our suffering
> Will turn into the wonders of the earth.

The last line in that poem reads: "Destiny is our friend."

## The Other Immigrant

A well known axiom: the United States of America is a "melting pot" of cultures. Whereas sophomoric thinking, conventional wisdom and public opinion suggest this is so, is it, in fact, a fallacy? Is the United States an immigrant heaven, where the immigrant discards her or his former self to start anew?

There are two kinds of immigrants: the tangible, the intangible. The one we readily know as an individual (or a family) who voluntarily journeys to and takes up residence in a foreign land. The intangibility of the other ensures it is not thought of as an immigrant; it is called: cosmogony.

Webster's Ninth New Collegiate Dictionary gives these, useful, definitions of cosmogony: (1) the creation or origin of the world or universe (2) a theory of the origin of the universe.

Facts on File, Inc.'s "Key Ideas in Human Thought", 1993, refers to cosmogony as Indigenous Metaphysics, and defines it:

> Indigenous Metaphysics describes conceptions among various peoples about the universe, the role of humans, and their relationship to unseen powers.

Implicit in these definitions: cosmogony is a story about Existence. And why, we might ask, do a people (a human being) need a cosmogony?

Humans' age old yearning to both comprehend and decipher meaning in Existence necessitated our need for a cosmogony. Consequently, since the beginning of Time, that is, since we became conscious of our existence, we have invented cosmogonies, told stories about Existence, in an attempt to answer the age old questions: What is the origin of the universe? Who are we? Why are we here? Is there a meaning and purpose for our existence? Is there life after death? How ought we to live?

The fundamental societal role of cosmogony is, therefore, both sacred and secular: It gives a people meaning in Existence. It is a practical, cultural necessity enabling a people to make sense of the world in which by no fault of its own it found itself; a psychological armor enabling it to fearlessly or less fearfully engage Existence, enabling it to exist and endure. It is from it a people derive its unique worldview, ethics and culture for social organization, without which a civil society will be problematic, perhaps altogether impossible.

Accordingly, besides the nominal definition of a people—the Berber; the Aborigine; the Yorùbá; the Igbo; the Masai; the Kikuyu; the Zulu; the Aztec; the Sioux; the "English"; the "French"; the "German"; the "American", et cetera—we also should understand a people as a society of human beings in a state of being. By a state of being I mean a way of life, which is itself derived from, and informed, influenced and ordered by that people's cosmogony, for a people is fundamentally its cosmogony, without which it will, like a tree sapped of nutrient, wither, die. (Consider these: it is not accidental that the faithful practitioner of Yorùbá reveres and worships her or his ancestors and the Òrìsàs. It is similarly not accidental that the faithful practitioner of Islam prays five times a day, does not consume pork, does not charge interest based on the market-principle of liberal economics. The faithful Yorùbá, and the faithful Muslim behave thus in accordance with the cardinal tenets of their respective cosmogonies, out of which derived their respective religions, ethics and way of life, and which informs and influences their earthly existence.)

It is not surprising then that cosmogony has been indispensable to human existence throughout all of known (recorded) human history. The Christian cosmogony in the Old Testament tells us: "In the beginning God created the heavens and the earth," and Adam and Eve, the first man and woman, and established the rules by which they were to live.

The cosmogony of our so called modern age we might call rational-scientific: a rational explanation of Existence through the use of Reason and the scientific method. Its cardinal tenet: the universe came into being as a result of a cosmic "Big Bang" and has been evolving ever since. And human beings are a result of a "glorious accident" of Nature, not an intentional act of creation by God.

All historical cosmogonies—including the biblical, those of the major religions of the world, of the Yorùbá, of the Zulu, et cetera—we might call pre modern. All of them are nowadays called "myth." This is not surprising: Our modern age is one where Reason increasingly informs and influences our worldviews and ways of life. The rational-scientific cosmogony claims superiority over the pre modern, because unlike them it does not merely tell us its version of the origin of the universe, of humans: it "proves" it with "convincing" scientific data. Regardless, we continue to wonder exactly what it was that banged. Why it had to bang. And why Matter had to eventually become conscious of Itself, be able to look at Itself in the highest most tangible and animated form of a human being. Moreover, we wonder about the (our) beginning. What did it look like? No one among us human beings remembers. (Do the stars, the planets, the moons?) It is as if we were plagued by a collective amnesia upon becoming conscious of our existence; as if in exchange for Consciousness, God (or call It whatever pleases you: "Nature", the "Big" that "banged", "Nothingness") struck us with a divine Wand, erasing our pre-conscious collective memory, leaving our collective unconscious devoid of any recollection of our pre-conscious, you might say, worry free Garden of Eden existence. And, given these vexing questions, we suspect the rational-scientific cosmogony is itself a "myth" because, despite its verifiability, it is, like pre modern cosmogonies, trying to explain Existence, and has not been able to conclusively answer humankind's age old questions: (No wonder physicists are questing for a grand theory, the so called theory of everything.)

It is revealing that human beings remain burdened with finding meaning in Existence: we have not fully accepted the "myth" of the rational-scientific cosmogony. And one wonders why this is so. Is it because we are innately atavistic and thus cannot help our being burdened with yearning to recollect the beginning, our primordial pre-conscious existence? Is it because we cannot help our being burdened with the inkling we are not merely the "glorious accident" of a cosmic "Big Bang"? Perhaps it is because we have come to believe we are indeed a "glorious accident," but cannot accept and be at peace with this explanation of our origin? Perhaps our being so burdened reveals our innate spirituality? . . .

A cosmogony is unique and localized to the people from whom it originated. Regardless, it does transcend its locality; missionaries, agents of government and immigrants are the primary conduits, the trans-planters. As the great writer, Ben Okri points out in his essay, "Redreaming the World":

> "The ancient Romans built straight roads wherever they went. Christians planted churches on resistant landscapes. Muslims pierce the air with the call of the muezzin.
>
> "Conquerors are transplanters. So are the conquered and exiles. They take their earth with them, carry with them their rituals as codes of continuity in the new world. [...]"

The age old capacity of immigrants for transplanting their cosmogonies to their new countries of residence is why one is skeptical about the idea of social integration believed as a "melting pot" into which dissolves the unique psychological interior and cultural traits of the immigrant when she or he takes up residence in her or his new country. Social integration understood as an incorporation of the immigrant into a "melting pot" is perhaps an illusion. It is perhaps more accurate to understand it as a conglomerating pot and not a melting pot of cultures; a hearty, spicy gumbo, not a bland puree of cultures. Consider this: the many peoples and cultures in New York City: pagans, Muslims, Christians, Jews, pantheists, atheists, rationalists, et cetera, and their respective unique cosmogonies, worldviews, cultures, social norms and institutions all coexisting, without melting one another. (There are neighborhoods throughout New York City with more religious-cultural affinities with Africa, the Middle East and South America than with the rest of the United States.) Moreover, these peoples and cultures are constantly engaged in a dynamic process of influencing one another, subtly vying for the hearts and minds of one another in the ongoing spiritual-cultural drama of Existence played out in cosmogonies and the ways of life derived from them. . . .

The foregoing leads me to this point:

Not only is a cosmogony an immigrant: the drama, often violent, of cosmogonies is what wholly and truly explains human history since we became conscious of our existence. Humans are the primary actors, the trans-planters of a cosmogony beyond its country of origin. And, cosmogony often wins human converts among the natives of the foreign lands to which it is transplanted. (Consider these: the proliferation of the Yorùbá cosmogony and way of life in the African Diaspora, most notably in the new world, including in the United States; the role of the British civil servants in the spreading of Britain's way of life in the colonies of the British Empire; the role of the missionaries in spreading Christianity in Africa, Asia and South America; the role of Arab traders and conquerors in spreading the Islamic faith and way of life in Africa.)

As Ben Okri points out in his essay, "Among the Silent Stones":

"Apart from the wounding of the souls of continents, colonialism also- paradoxically- achieved an accidental serendipity. It brought people together in a way that might not have happened for hundreds of years. For example, as a result of its over-reaching, Britain began by colonising half the world and now finds half the world in its territory, within its history, subtly altering its psyche."

The altering of psyche Okri mentions relates to, of course, the influence the unique ways of life of immigrants are having on the people and life of Britain. (Perhaps politicians who detest immigrants are not only hatemongers but have mused on and comprehended the profound life-altering influence of the immigrants' cosmogonies on the people and life of their countries and thus are fearful of foreign cultural influence, of change.)

A cosmogony ought to be understood as an immigrant given its intrinsic ability to migrate beyond its land of origin through human immigrants, whose inner universe and behavior it continues to influence in the new country. This is especially so, given its ability to influence the worldview and way of life of the indigenous persons of the country to which it is transplanted, and, consequently, the life of country itself.

Has the immensity of the United States, the relative peaceful cohabitation of its diverse cultures and peoples meant it has achieved a "melting pot" of cultures, or is this an illusion, a self fulfilling axiom?

## The March of History amid Us

Aromatic tobacco, red wine and music were my sole sources of light throughout those days of my black hole of an existence. I would stay in my living room chain smoking, drinking, listening to Beethoven, Chopin, Sun Ra, Miles, Coltrane, Felá, intermittently pacing the floor like a caged lion.

It was the period in my life when I had become disillusioned with academia. I had uncovered its inability to impart knowledge, its destiny being, I had finally comprehended, social engineering. I, therefore, had decided to abandon it as my guide at knowledge seeking.

My spirit enchanted by the magic of Spring, one particularly lovely spring day during that period I decided to go walking about New York City, people watching. I felt good, having recently overcome my bluesy existence, and resolved to thenceforth play the lone detective in my search for Knowledge. My intention was to aimlessly walk about the city, starting at its southernmost end, the Staten Island Ferry Terminal, and walk northward as far as I could endure. It was on that day I encountered the statues, those magical statues, in front of the "Old Custom House."

The "Old Custom House" is situated at the foot of Broadway, the southernmost district of the city. Adorning the front of the building are the statues, four of them, massive. They would come to dominate my thought for years, a measure of their irresistible charm on me.

A huge building this "Old Custom House" is. A long wide staircase leads to its main entrance. Atop the staircase is an archway; on a big banner hung underneath the bowed entrance of the archway is written: "The National Smithsonian Museum of the American Indian."

As you stand on the street-level facing the building, you see the statues lining its frontal length: two in its middle, flanking the staircase, one at its right outer corner, one at its left outer corner.

The statue at the right outer corner of the building portrays a voluptuous, sultry woman in slumber, her perky breasts exposed to the world. Her head drops to her side, her left hand rests on the head of a lion sprawled belly-down at her feet; its eyes closed in sleep, her right hand rests on the head of the Sphinx. And behind her is a draped figure whose face is somewhat hidden.

The next statue portrays a stern-faced woman, a crown on her head, a breastplate engraved with esoteric symbols covering her torso. Her left hand, the fingers clenched into a fist, rests on a book atop a globe depicting the world, behind which sits a cloaked figure reading a book. Behind her is the prow of a ship, from which protrudes what looks like a warhead. Beside the ship is a lion and, barely visible, the head of a jackal (or is it the head of a bull) and a grotesque eagle-headed figure, its beak curved. Visible behind her is an eagle, its wings somewhat unfolded.

The next statue portrays a woman looking boldly ahead of her. She holds a torch in her right hand and a cloak in her left hand over the head of a kneeling figure, behind the figure is another seated figure reading, it seems. On her lap rests a bountiful sheaf, and behind her are an eagle and the figure of an American Indian gazing into the distance.

The next and last statue portrays a woman on a throne, a crown on her head. She sits with her eyes closed, holding a lotus flower between her right thumb and middlefinger, both of which she touches together in a manner suggesting she is meditating. A serpent is wound round the stem of the flower. On her lap sits a miniature statue of Buddha. Underneath her feet are human skulls. On her left hand side are men bowing to her as if acknowledging her majesty, surrendering to her will. On her right hand side sits an upright tiger. Behind her, right at the back of her head, blocked from a frontal view of her, is a cross. The eerie aura of all the statues is stronger in this statue in particular, which is somewhat terrifying to look at for long, especially when you gaze at the woman's face, her eyes closed in meditation. Of all the statues, I was that day and today remain most drawn to this one.

What I had planned as a daylong walkabout the city

ended with the statues. I had left them and gone to a nearby coffee shop and mused on them. Since then they had prowled in my thought, prompting my visiting the building many more times to gaze at them from the comfort of a bench chair at the Bowling Green Park situated across the building.

Utterly intriguing the statues are; magnetic their charm on my thought, my emotion. I would sometimes visit them at night, their eeriness more intense at this time of day. I knew intuitively they tell a hidden story. So intense was my desire to decipher their story that, eventually, I decided to do the inevitable.

My endeavor to uncover the hidden story the statues tell led me to literature on them; some of which were sent to me or handed to me by friends and acquaintances sympathetic to my "noble" mission. It was thus I began to accumulate information about the statues.

What I "learned" about the statues in the literature I read on them I immediately suspected were merely informational: The Custom House was the center of commerce for the United States. In the early twentieth century most of the income of the entire government of the United States came from custom duties. The location of the Custom House close to New York Harbor is symbolic of and reinforces its importance to America's economic wellbeing. Cass Gilbert was the architect of the building. Daniel Chester French, chosen by Gilbert to "adorn" the ("his") building, was the sculptor of the statues. . . .

I have many times heard tour guides regurgitate that information about the statues to clusters of tourists in front of the building. Sometimes during the tour guides' fervent regurgitation, they offer pointers, somewhat, to the tourists about the hidden story the statues tell. As when a particularly excited (or perhaps dedicated) tour guide would tell the tourists the statues "indeed" portray the four continents of Asia, Africa, Europe and America. That the statues portray the four continents I had found out in the literature I read on them. And it was on this particular information I had increasingly concentrated my musing on the statues, incessantly thinking about voluptuous, sultry

Africa deep in slumber, as is the lion sprawled at her feet, the Sphinx magnificent beside her; about stern faced Europe, an ageing queen, looking as if she had been wronged and was bent on revenge; about exuberant America, looking boldly ahead of her, eager to confront the world, and about majestic, sacred Asia, on whose lap sits Buddha, the cross erect at the back of her head, men bowing in deference to her, human skulls beneath her feet.

Yes, the statues portray the four continents, but what about them? (I believe deceptive all the information extant on this question.) What is the real meaning of the statues, what are they really concealing or revealing? This question nagged me.

. . .

Playing the lone detective at knowledge seeking, I have come to realize, is wretched business, devastating, destabilizing and a sure path to "lunacy." Knowledge only belongs to the gods. (The Dead know it, but they are dead, and, therefore, not readily accessible to the living, the human being in search of Knowledge.) Only the initiated human being provided the clues with which to decipher esoteric symbols, the divine mode of communication of the gods, can attain Knowledge. Still, I keep thinking about the statues. (Perhaps the Dead would in time be impressed by and reward my devotion to and tenacity at knowledge seeking.)

After innumerable sunrises, sunsets and moons of musing on and visiting the statues I now know they captured my imagination because they tell an earth shattering story. I continue to have an intense hunch it is a coded, cosmic story; the age-old conundrum of a story which explains much about, perhaps the entirety of, the march of History amid us.

## The Two Kinds of Persons

It seems to me there are two kinds of persons: the philosophic natured and the non philosophic natured.

Of those I call philosophic natured persons, some are historical, others, many of them less known, are extant. The historical ones I know only through their works and works on them. I am fortunate to know personally some of the extant ones, others I know only through their works and works on them.

Who are those I call philosophic natured persons? The question ought to be: What does it mean to be philosophic natured?

Three words are essential: Philosophic, Nature, Natured. You will find in a decent dictionary useful definition of these words; here are those in mine:

> Philosophic: Pertaining to or founded on the principles of philosophy (Philosophy being the love of wisdom as leading to the search for it; hence, knowledge of general principles—elements, powers, or causes and laws—as explaining facts and existences); Self-restrained and serene; rational; thoughtful; calm. Philosophic also refers to the calm judgement and equable temper resulting from the study of causes and laws; practical wisdom; fortitude—ability to endure reverses and suffering.
>
> Nature: The character, constitution, or essential traits of a person, thing, or class, especially if original rather than acquired; The physical or psychic constitution or character of persons or things, whether native or acquired.

Natured: Possessing a nature, disposition, or temperament.

A philosophic natured person can, therefore, be usefully defined thus: The person who possesses and demonstrates the principles of philosophy, who loves wisdom and endeavors to be wise, who possesses and demonstrates calm judgment, practical wisdom and endurance and who is self-restrained, calm, rational and thoughtful.

I have read about and observed in PNPs certain traits, so that I have come to believe in some of the essential traits of PNPs:

They are conscious—by this I mean they have discerning awareness of the forces influencing their society. They are contemplatively natured. They are steadfast in their devotion to (seeking) Knowledge and detest ignorance. They stimulate thought. They are inclined toward the spiritual not the material. They are decisively influenced by content, not form. They are drawn to aimless wandering, whereby they walk about contemplating, often incessantly, the world about them. They love freedom and detest domination. They are incessant thinkers. They appreciate chance encounters. They are humble. Love energizes their being . . . PNPs are in the minority of human beings.

I am not suggesting that to be a PNP the person must possess all these traits, nor do I intend them to be complete. I think of it like this: the degree of a person's philosophic naturedness will be determined by how many of the traits that person possesses.

> Who are those I call non philosophic natured persons (NPNPs), or what does it mean to be non philosophic natured?

NPNPs are not conscious—they not only lack discerning awareness of the forces affecting their society, they are not disposed to thinking about such matters. They are not given to contemplation. They usually are ignorant and are not necessarily eager to seek Knowledge. They do not necessarily stimulate thought. They are inclined toward the material not the spiritual. They often are decisively influenced by form not content. They are not given to incessant thinking. They do not necessarily appreciate chance encounters. They are not necessarily humble. They usually do not let Love energize their being . . . NPNPs are in the majority of human beings.

You are probably shaking your head in disagreement, thinking: How can he be so narrow minded, his worldview so dichotomous? Is everything so black and white? I do appreciate your sentiment. And I think it is quite possible you might, after your initial reaction, come to think favorably of my seemingly judgmental, "narrow minded" division of persons into two broad categories when you consider this:

PNPs are often "unhappy" people. Happiness is one human preoccupation they do not bother with. (What is "happiness," really?) Their life is one of struggle and pain because they are not and cannot be satisfied with the state—the so called "reality"—-of the world. They cannot because they know this to be true: That "reality" is manmade and is usually based on selfishness, greed, ruthless social engineering, half truths, manufactured truths and lies, all sustained by organized ingenious modes of domination, sometimes by outright force. PNPs know this. And, no, they cannot be satisfied with it. Their nature compels them not to be satisfied with it. They have a discerning sense, a sense of other possibilities: that which concerns human beings universally. They know all human beings constitute one extended family. They, therefore, are necessarily interested in and devoted to that which will realize justice for all human beings; that which is based on truth not lies; that which is based on freedom not domination; that which seeks to elevate human beings to their true stature inherent in their true nature. PNPs have comprehended this true nature of human beings to be this: Human beings are embryonic gods and have the ability to create endless possibilities. Their comprehension of the true nature of human being is why PNPs value progress, why the desire for it propels them, why they are steadfastly devoted to it.

The custodians of the status quo of a society—those at the helm of the power structure of a society, whose aim is to maintain their privileged positions, and who usually are NPNPs—detest change and, consequently, deny any idea or action aiming to actualize it. And given that PNPs are visionaries striving to engender change, they aim to and do rouse people. They, therefore, betray themselves as a threat to the continuity of the privileged positions of the custodians. That is why the custodians seek to extinguish the revolutionary fire of the ideas of PNPs. And they often succeed. One was nailed to the cross; another was handed a poison to ingest; still another was fatally shot on the veranda of a building. Many others are today ostracized, harassed, goaded into poverty, threatened, jailed, about to be murdered.

. . .

I suspect you are wondering what explains why some persons are philosophic natured and others are not.

It is a question I have long contemplated. My emergent thought on it is this (it contradicts, seemingly, what I have written thus far): Philosophic nature is inherent in the human being, so all human beings have the ability to be philosophic. To use a technological term, the Hardware needed to make a human being a PNP is innate in all human beings, Culture provides the Software (the Software is the Culture). Therefore, Culture—understood as the social heart of a society, which sustains and guides its persons—is the single most important factor which nurtures or neglects (influences) the innate philosophic naturedness of a human being.

Although philosophic nature is inherent in the human being, it has been undermined in the majority of human beings by the pressure of living, in particular living in this age of modernity, whose spirit of fluid morals rules modern life, whose reason for being, whose God is Money. The philosophical impulse, therefore, must be (re)nurtured in the majority of human beings.

To have a righteous world, a world where human beings are unfettered in mind and spirit and thus are able to live a life energized by Love, able to fully actualize their godly nature to create endless possibilities, able to live a fulfilling life free of the (social) plague of greed, selfishness, apathy, anomie, neuroses, and psychoses humanity needs to be reconciled with its inherent philosophic nature. How that is to achieved remains the vexing question. Encouraging a culture that nourishes it is fundamental. But would a society where such a culture endures and flourishes survive in this world?

## The Thoughts of a Man Who Recently Reunited with His Destiny
(Invented)

> The reality of what we are doing to one another is explosive. The secret content of our lives is terrifying. There is much to scream about. There are great pollulating lies and monsters running around in the seabed of our century. [...]
>
> Something is needed to wake us from the frightening depths of our moral sleep.
>
> Ben Okri, "The Human Race Is Not Yet Free."

This essay is my endeavor to contribute a critical thought on Gidaland. I do so in hope this plagued land might be healed.

Before I begin may I humbly suggest you charmingly beg your wife, husband, girlfriend, boyfriend, sons, or daughters to allow you some time to be alone. And pour yourself a mug of tea or coffee, a glass of wine or, my favorite, cognac, and tuck yourself into bed, prop your head with fluffy pillows. Or recline your reading chair; push yourself comfortably into your sofa. Whichever one is your habit or desire. And surrender yourself to my thoughts, the thoughts of a man who recently reunited with his destiny. I promise you it will not take too long. You should tell your family this; it will help ensure they leave you alone and undisturbed for the time it will take to read. And let me say this beforehand. In this age where time to nurture the mind or the spirit is increasingly scarce, I thank you, and your family too, for allotting some of your precious time to read my essay.

I would like to begin by acknowledging that this essay benefited tremendously from numerous conversations with Òdodo, Gidaland's foremost man of letters, regarding Gidaland's tribulation in particular, the human condition in general. Moreover, his writings have profoundly affected me, and inspired and greatly informed this essay; specifically, his thoughtful essay, The *Two Kinds of Persons*.

I begin with notes on myself.

I am a man who recently achieved a self-transformation and thereby reunited myself with my destiny as indicated by my name.

My name, Jéjélayé, roughly translates: gentle, the life (live life gently). In our culture we believe a name suggests the innate nature of the bearer, and this nature will manifest in his or her earthly demeanor. Thus, implicit in my name is this: I was destined to be a happy-go-lucky, humble person. My earthly demeanor as the dictatorial ruler of Gidaland, an actor in the drama of global domination (popularly called, international politics) all these years clearly proves I had abandoned my destiny. But that is in the past, for, as I say, I have reunited with my destiny.

For some time, more so since my transformation, I have been intensely reflective. At no point in my life have I been so intellectually challenged. My pondering led to an itchy desire to offer my thoughts on the agonizing human condition in Gidaland, one result of which is this essay.

Although my name is Jéjélayé, They call me the "Sphinx." Who are they? I use they as a collective designation for those who call themselves Gidaland's intellectuals. Their self-imposed calling is to engage in social criticism. They accuse me of being a despot. They call me a Beast. They say I am immoral, ruthless, selfish, cunning, domineering . . . They say I am abusing my power by hindering the freedom of our people, their human rights, their dreams, causing them great suffering. They say I am mismanaging Gidaland's affairs and finances, enriching my allies and myself in the process. They say I have engendered a society plagued with widespread corruption, economic mismanagement, political fraud, lawlessness . . . Nothing that happens in Gidaland misses their criticism. Being intellectuals, and having appointed themselves promoters of Freedom and public spiritedness, I suppose they have the right to present their thoughts on Gidaland's socio-economic-political and ethical life.

I am not disputing their accusations. I am guilty of all they accuse me. I acknowledge they are doing the moral thing by denouncing me for my dictatorial leadership and deplorable deeds. What I disagree with is their identifying me as the cause of Gidaland's plagued existence because what that essentially means is this: they are accusing me of being the clog in Gidaland's wheels of progress. And in that respect, they are mistaken, grossly mistaken. Nothing could be further from the truth. It is a critical mistake to think me an impediment to Gidaland's progress. Why do I believe so?

The truth of the matter is I am a symptom of Gidaland's social illness, not its cause. And, immoral I am not. I am a man of God. I admit I have not always allowed my sense of morality to inform my thoughts and influence my actions. It is true I am cunning and ruthless in my dealings with our people, be they civilians, or civic-minded members of the Military. How else is one to ensure obedience, and preserve one's rule? How else is one to deal with opponents who refuse the riches one is willing to bestow on them? What better way to deal with them if not by crushing them? Cruelty becomes one's most reliable ally; one is compelled to fully utilize it. Cruelty, will and caprice are indispensable traits of a despotic leader; without them he cannot survive. (And I should mention this: we often fail to point out, especially when denouncing despots, that we all have the innate capacity for those traits.) A despotic leader, by definition, must be cruel, he must be able to assert and execute his will and caprice in order to silence the opposition and to keep his people fearful. Our intellectuals should have pondered and realized this is what a despot does, what a despot is compelled to do to survive. They should have understood that, to maintain the domination of his people, instilling fear in them is indispensable to a despot. And what is a better way to instill fear in one's people if not ruling willfully, capriciously, cruelly?

Gidaland's intellectuals are highly educated, and well-informed. They comprise writers, social critics, lawyers, judges, university professors . . . Accordingly, one would think they are familiar with writings on the issue of despotism and despots, and realize that I, a despot, am able to rule Gidaland despotically because it is a despotic country, a jungle. (It has not always been so. I will explain what I mean shortly.) And because it is unthinkable they are not familiar with literature on despotism and despots, I must conclude they have opted to ignore such work. That would explain why they always espouse passionate criticisms that identify me as the cause of Gidaland's plagued existence, which, essentially, amounts to shallow thinking, babbling, a fervent display of passion to "right the wrong" in Gidaland.

Besides identifying me as the cause of Gidaland's problems and denouncing me for them, Gidaland's intellectuals, and foreign critics of Africa, wrongly affirm these are what impede Africa's development: corruption, tribalism, nepotism, military dictatorship, (assumed) lack of democracy, controlled-economies . . . That is simply not true. Besides military regimes, African countries have "democratic" governments. Where has it led us? It has led us backward not forward; we are regressing not progressing. And dare I say nepotism, corruption, controlled-economy are extant in many countries and governments all over the world, even in prosperous Europe and North America. . . .

So, Gidaland's intellectuals are greatly mistaken. My rejoinder to their criticisms of me is this: Wake up! Revolutionize your thoughts! Start thinking profoundly! Why? Because your thoughts are shallow, no more than a passionate display of your sense of justice, no more than a showy display of your intellectual ability. What do I mean by "thinking profoundly"? It is time you realize I am not Gidaland's fundamental enemy. It is time you realize I am not the clog in Gidaland's wheels of progress. Nor are the factors that foreign critics of Africa affirm. I say to you, and your peers all over the world who have made African Affairs their area of focus: it is time all of you realize Gidaland's fundamental enemy. Africa's fundamental enemy is invisible but nonetheless real, like a deadly virus hidden deep within the body, slowly consuming it. It is time all of you realize Gidaland's fundamental enemy; the intangible but nonetheless real enemy of its progress; the real clog in its wheels of progress; the non-material deadly virus consuming it is its historical reality. It has made a jungle of Gidaland; it explains its dog-eat-dog existence.

Gidaland's historical reality and its role in making Gidaland a jungle of a society is the thought provoking issue Gidaland's intellectuals and their peers all over the world should have raised, and be pondering rather than squandering their intellectual energy denouncing me, advocating my removal from Gidaland's leadership, proclaiming it must be done "at all cost because historically despots have not been known to relinquish power without the ardent struggle of the people." My dear critics seem not to comprehend Gidaland's historical reality engendered its plagued existence. All they do is criticize me. They delight in arguing for my demise as the panacea for ending Gidaland's suffering, as if all would be well if I were to abdicate leadership, and we were to institute a "democratic" government forthwith. . . .

Let me now discuss what I mean by Gidaland's historical reality and how its jungle existence is explained by it.

Because it is fundamental to human existence I begin with the issue of worldview.

As Òdodo in our heady conversations and in his writings often refers to it, by worldview I mean the cosmogony-cosmology of a people, which Òdodo often calls a story. I prefer to call it a worldview; they are essentially the same. When Òdodo says a people is the Story it tells itself about Existence he means a people is essentially its worldview. That is, the story that people tell to explain the origin of the universe, to make sense of the world. I totally agree with him.

From the vantage point of today, we now know, should know, this: the worldview of a people is the root of that people's culture. The worldview of a people is that which informs, influences and orders that people's way of life—the visible social, economic, political philosophies, and ethics and religion of that society. The Way of Life is the visible superstructure, the worldview is the invisible substructure that holds and supports it, without which it will collapse. Here is a useful illustration:

Way of Life (visible)
Worldview (invisible)

Therefore, a worldview should also be understood as a psychological armor that enables a people to engage Existence, to live, to endure. It should be understood as a practical and cultural necessity that identifies and maintains a people as a cultural entity, informs and influences its existence, and from which it derives its unique culture and ethics for organizing its society, without which society is impossible.

From the vantage point of today we also now know, should know, this: the battle of worldviews is what wholly and truly explains human history to date. . . .

Human beings (a people) need a worldview so as to make sense of the world, to endure. The people of Gidaland are, of course, no exception to this. Therefore, we have indigenous worldview regarding how the world came to be, the nature of God, the relation of God to Man and His relationship with Man, the nature of Man, what the destiny of Man is, how he must live, the relationship of man to man, what constitutes the "good life" . . . It is our indigenous worldview that used to inform, influence and order our indigenous way of life that we derived from it.

In light of the foregoing idea of worldview I now turn to a discussion of its relevance to Gidaland's historical reality and how its jungle existence is explained by it.

A jungle has its operative logic that informs, influences, and orders its existence. Willfulness, selfishness, cunningness, cruelty, caprice are prevailing traits in the jungle. They are the jungle's operative traits, the behavioral foundation of its existence. Their prevalence exposes the precariousness of survival in the jungle. . . .

A country where despots and despotism thrives is a territory tantamount to a jungle. Thus, a system of overt and covert despotism caused and maintained by fear, insecurity and self-preservation, and an inclination for control reign supreme in such a country. Therefore, blaming a person in such a country as responsible for the jungle existence, as our intellectuals do me, betrays a lack of understanding of the workings of the jungle. . . .

Gidaland today is a jungle, although it has not always been so. The majority of those with whom, and those through whom, I rule Gidaland have jungle mentality—myself included, of course, but that was before my transformation. Their traits are those of the jungle. They are willful, selfish, cruel, cunning, corrupt and capricious. All are indispensable traits in our business of domination in the jungle territory, the dog-eat-dog, the Darwinian society Gidaland is, and in which our distressed people live, struggling daily to stay alive.

How did Gidaland become a jungle?

Gidaland is a society in transition. By transition I mean a period in which a society shifts from its indigenous worldview and the way of life derived from it to a foreign worldview and way of life. The transition could be willed from within the society itself or imposed by external agents. The indigenous societies of Africa, Asia, North America, South America, Australia and the South Seas are examples of societies whose ongoing transition was imposed by external agents/ factors—their so called discovery by Europe.

It is in a society's transitional phase that the jungle comes into being, then flourishes and proliferates. . . .

For Gidaland, the transition occurred from one of a society founded on a harmonious, indigenous worldview—the "animistic"-magico-religious worldview—to the cacophonous one of today, in which the remains of our indigenous, "animistic" worldview exists alongside a trio of foreign worldviews: the Islamic, the Christian, the "rational-scientific." The transition was not willed and induced by our people, but willed and imposed cunningly, brutally by the outside world. . . .

Gidaland became a jungle when the outside world "discovered" it. That is what I mean by Gidaland's historical reality. Gidaland's jungle existence today is the sad reality its contact with the outside world has made of it.

The outside world "discovered" Gidaland and set about supplanting our indigenous worldview from which we had derived our indigenous culture, and in accordance with which we had organized our indigenous way of life, which had sustained us for millennia. That effectively ended our erstwhile autonomous existence. It was a three-pronged attack. The Arabs told us their Islamic worldview, and, with the sharp edges of their swords grazing our throats, forcibly converted a multitude of our people to the Islamic faith. The Occidentals deemed us barbarian, idol worshippers; their "Christian missionaries" told us their Christian worldview and cunningly, brutally converted a multitude of our people to the Christian faith. Their secular counterparts, the "scientific explorers," exploited, and continue to exploit our natural resources. Contrary to their claim, they did not introduce us to science and the scientific method; they introduced us to their "rational-scientific" worldview. (They did not introduce us to science because long before the Occidentals "discovered" us, our ancestors were science-literate and were master-practitioners of the Trial and Error process characteristic of the scientific method, the distinguishing characteristic of which is collecting data, analyzing it and deducing Knowledge from the process. That Africans were a millennium ago smelting iron in internal combustion furnaces to produce iron implements is one example that testifies to this. Many more examples abound if you care to investigate ancient civilizations in Africa.)

With the systematic inculcation of the Islamic, the Christian and the "rational-scientific" worldviews in our people, our indigenous worldview and way of life—our Lifeline—was forcibly displaced, tactlessly cut off and replaced with those of the foreign worldviews. They made Allah and Jesus Christ and Reason our new God. They disrobed us and attired us in caftans and turbans. Attired us in white robes and crucifixes. Attired us in suffocating suits and ties. They gave us new names. Koranic names. Biblical names. Named us after their names for the days of the week, astrological names: Sunday, Monday, Friday. They twisted our tongues with their language. They bended our minds, re-oriented our thought processes and thinking, our sense of justice, morality and fair play. Thus, we became cultural-amphibians. They turned us against one another. Brothers fought and conquered brothers. Sisters yelled and spat at sisters. Sons disobeyed mothers. Daughters disobeyed fathers. Mothers, the pillar of our existence, were deposed from their rightful place at the head of the family, accused of being temptresses, ordered to conceal themselves from neck to ankle, relegated to the back room, the kitchen, ordered to serve men thenceforth, and thus they invented Women. They replaced our indigenous shrines with mosques, and with churches. They replaced our oral tradition, whereby our customs, and our knowledge of the world were passed on from the old to the young, with their written tradition and through it taught their customs and knowledge of the world to us in "colleges." They replaced our hands-on approach to acquiring skills, whereby our trades and crafts were taught by our masters to apprentices, with "technical schools" where they taught us their trades and crafts. They replaced our communal courtyards with member-only country clubs. They replaced our judicial system with the court of Sharia Law, the court of Confession and the court of "Rational" Law. (I recall Chinua Achebe's novel, *Things Fall Apart.*) They hoarded and shipped to Europe innumerable of our pantheons and cultural artifacts which embody our indigenous worldview, tell our history and testify to our glorious ancient civilization. Many of them would later show up in museums in Europe and North America, and in the homes of many of their famous and wealthy people. I recall Ben Okri's poem, "Lament of the Images"; especially this stanza:

They took some images
And brought them across
The whitening seas
And stored them in
Basements
For later study
Of the African's
Dark and impenetrable
Mind.
They called them 'Primitive objects'
And subjected them
To the milk

Of scientific
Scrutiny.

What theft! What sacrilege! What barbarity! . . .

Their cultural imperialism was merely a stage in their destruction of our indigenous existence, in their destruction of our life. In time, innumerable people were stolen, hoarded and shackled like lambs and shipped across the sea to nourish the so called new world.

And having been robbed of our spiritual essence, our indigenous civilization undermined, defeated, those of us left became demoralized. Our psyche maimed, we were no longer able to understand ourselves, and the new world in which we found ourselves.

With no indigenous worldview, Everything is up for grabs. Such a society becomes a jungle where anything goes, where only the strong survive, where fear, greed, corruption, tribalism, nepotism, cruelty, domination are prevalent, where the worst in human beings is cultivated, nourished, flourished and manifested in its people's demeanor, eventually enabling an outsider to objectively, innocently, say of them: "That is who they are"; "That is how they are." This is the society Gidaland has become.

If Gidaland's jungle existence is not transformed another despotic leader will surely follow me as many are waiting for their turn to dominate her for their own emotional pleasure and material gain. . . .

That is not surprising as a jungle society is most conducive to the creation and proliferation of jungle men. As a political leader, the jungle man embodies the worst in human beings. He is selfish, greedy, corrupt and insecure. He is averse to morality. He believes life is a struggle for existence; that only the strong survive. In his jungle, survival of the fittest mentality, the fittest man is the most powerful man, that is to say, the absolute ruler. His main preoccupation is self-preservation. Accordingly, although he is capable of moral choice, he must be amoral. Morality is not one of his codes of conduct. And because he is not moral, he is not civil. His interest is not to live in a civil society, or to foster one. He is content to exist in the jungle and is, therefore, compelled to ensure the preservation of the jungle. And that is most assured via sheer power. Unmitigated power is therefore, essential to him. He thrives on it because he must be able to assert himself; he must be able to realize his will and caprice. He cannot concern himself with the progress of his society. So, like the beast in the jungle, he obeys his appetite. Whim, will, selfishness, indulgence, cunningness, and the use of force and absolute power are practical traits that define him and are indispensable to him. Tribalism, nepotism, bribery are useful means facilitating his endless quest at self-preservation through domination, strengthening and fostering his jungle existence. He, the jungle man, should be understood akin to the non philosophic man. . . .

I totally agree with Òdodo's idea that societies today are inhabited by two kinds of men: the philosophic and the non philosophic. I also agree with him that the majority of men are of the non philosophic kind. Here we find man living an unexamined life. Emulation has become his norm. He follows in others' footsteps. To be like others, to win favorable public opinion informs and influences his conduct. He does not bother to think profoundly about his life. He does not bother to reflect on his conduct and the adverse effect it might have had, might be having, on his society. Anyone who so reflects, he believes, is an idealist, which he is not because he "knows" that "things are the way they are, and one must take life as such." He lusts after power and prestige, and will do anything to gain it. But that is not so with the philosophic man. . . .

Although the philosophic man is often in the minority, he is the true mover and shaker of events in the world. His philosophic nature makes him a perpetual thinker. He seeks Knowledge. He seeks to comprehend the world. He is the one conscious of possibilities others are unaware of; the one who see things others do not. He encourages others to partake of the philosophic life because he believes, rightly, it is important that all are knowledge seeking. A state of being that can be attained only by way of philosophy, which simply means keeping the Life of the Mind perpetually receptive and engaged in thought. His, to be sure, is the noblest of endeavors. (What endeavor is nobler than the pursuit of Knowledge?) He is perpetually in love with humanity, which for him is not an abstract idea but a living reality made of flesh and blood, in need of spiritual and material nourishment, and imbued with the capacity for endless possibilities, divine abilities. So, he seeks to elevate humanity to its divine height. He uses, among others, oration, literature, music, film to affect humanity so that the world might be justly or more justly organized. . . .

Although now and then the philosophic man triumphantly challenges the prevailing power of his society, his steadfast tendency for knowledge seeking and his non-conformist methods of knowing counters prevalent mores and attitudes. And because he is often in the minority and usually not in a position of power, therefore, defenseless against tyranny, he often falls prey to injustice. He is often intentionally charged and convicted of crimes and silenced so as to suppress his revolutionary fervor and thus neutralize its radiating influence on others. When the philosophic man is not murdered out-right, he is relentlessly harassed, jailed, ostracized, impoverished and goaded to lunacy. Those are some of the means of extinguishing his revolutionary fire of ideas; some of the means of undermining his message; some of the means of ending his wailing for personal and societal transformation, his wailing for Truth, Justice and Universal Love in the world. Philosophic man is concentrated energy, spawning a world of ideas. He cannot be annihilated. So, when he is murdered he lives on through his work. Accordingly, he is, rightly, called immortal.

The foregoing is my paraphrase (not without some plagiarism) of Òdodo's idea that the philosophic and the non philosophic are the two kinds of persons living today, which he cogently discussed in his appropriately famous essay: *The Two Kinds of Persons*. His ingenuity is revealed and immortalized in that essay. I appreciate the essay because it provides a profound yardstick to measure human beings. The essay enabled me to know of Òdodo as an intellectual worthy of the name before he became an international affairs journalist, the correspondent who covers my office for the Ecumenical Society. The essay intensely affected me. My self-transformation was roused and propelled by it.

I was a non philosophic man, a jungle man. A critical understanding of Gidaland was not on my list of concerns. I usually did not reflect on trans-personal issues. When I did reflect, it was never out of societal concern as I was not concerned about the wellbeing of our people. It was always for personal reasons: to contrive the endless maneuverings needed to realize whatever objective I desired to achieve; to contrive ways of decreeing cunning political and harsh economic policies that are often forced on me by the lords of the world; to contrive ways of crushing dissidents, manufacturing or buying consent; to contrive ways of forever instilling fear. . . .

That is not surprising because in a jungle country, political power, especially when it is absolute, allows the leader to have a merchant mentality. The non philosophic, power drunk leader is most likely to think of his country as a for-profit entity. Accordingly, he is most likely to conduct it as one conducts a business. He is most likely to become averse to morality. Selfishness, cunningness, cruelty are his indispensable traits. He deems his country's wealth a fruit-filled cake. He consumes most of it with those comprising the custodians of the status quo, whose interest and preservation is his duty to maintain, and shares the rest among those in his inner circle whose allegiance is necessary for the preservation of his domination. That the majority of his people are denied their share of the national cake is not a concern of his. This is the psychology of a non philosophic man, the man with jungle mentality, the Darwinian man, the man I was before my transformation. . . .

Why am I now writing this essay? Why am I now an earnest crusader for the transformation of Gidaland?

The answer is simple. I am free of the spell of Evil that has long demonized me. I have reconciled myself with my destiny as indicated in my name.

What specifically explains my self-transformation

(which I like to call change of heart and character)?

These two reasons are major:

I conquered death, and self-preservation:

By this I mean I made peace with death, and, consequently, self-preservation. It really was not difficult to do. As Òdodo often tells me in our conversations, no one can negate death. So, one has no choice but to live. Life is precious. It is in life that we can experience the manifold pleasures and pains of being alive. Therefore, one ought to appreciate life and live fully, and, ought to promote that which makes life meaningful not only for oneself but for others as well. It is crucial one comprehends this and its many connotations. It means one ought to promote Truth, Justice, Freedom, Knowledge, Love, brotherly love . . . If you see someone being abused you ought to do the best you can to stop it. If you meet someone sad you ought to give them comfort to the best of your ability. If you meet someone hungry and tired you ought to feed and give them rest to the best of your ability. You ought to promote love of Knowledge. You ought to strive to impart knowledge to the ignorant . . . heaven is an ideal to be realized here on earth. . . .

My friendship with Òdodo, his ideas and writings, and the world of ideas he introduced me to, and the philosophic fervor that had infused me upon reading his essay, *The Two Kinds of Persons*, intensified:

Consciously musing about one's society, and the world in general, and studying what eminent men of letters have taught and written about the human condition best appeases philosophic fervor. Philosophic fervor usually manifests in one's desire for Knowledge, for a deeper understanding of one's society, for a critical understanding of the affairs of this world, for self-transformation . . .

Having overcome my evil tendency, I detested myself for my deplorable deeds all these years as Gidaland's despotic ruler. Guilt relentlessly tormented me. I eventually sought solace in Literature—undoubtedly man's most powerful ally in his earnest pondering upon Existence—and began to muse incessantly on Gidaland's plight, on human existence.

Following a list Òdodo prepared for me, of the literature I have read so far I am most fascinated by that of Leo Tolstoy and Ben Okri. For someone who had not been concerned about Morality but who now sees its crucial importance to social organization, to human progress, the work of Tolstoy and Okri made me see the world in a different light, as it could be. As Òdodo often tells me in our conversations, I started thinking seriously and came to believe that heaven could exist right here on earth, that the realization of Universal Freedom here on earth is the ultimate goal.

Citing the moral crisis of his life, Tolstoy divided his life into four periods. The third and fourth periods perfectly describe mine. The third was an eighteen-year period from his marriage to his "spiritual birth," during which he lived "a proper, honest" family life, "not yielding to vices castigated by public opinion" which characterized his second twenty year period "of vulgar licentiousness, of ambition-serving, vainglory and, chiefly, lust." The fourth was a twenty-year period, in which he hoped to die, and from the vantage point of which he comprehended the significance of his life. He would alter nothing about his life, he said, except the "evil habits" he previously acquired.

As Tolstoy in his third and fourth periods, I am reborn in spirit, living a pious life, a life of vision for a just future for Gidaland, my main regret being my erstwhile evil deeds. I have mentally relinquished my despotic ways, my jungle mentality. My life is laid bare before me, its importance clear to me. I now know how I must live and what I must do henceforth. (My transformation is yet to manifest in concrete political action to transform Gidaland. But it soon will!)

Okri's literature should be in the library of anyone who cares about the wellbeing of human beings. He engages in a passionate prayer for Truth, for Justice, for Knowledge, for Love, for brotherly love in the world, for human survival at this troubled juncture in human existence. His essay, "While the World Sleeps" speaks directly to my heart. I am like the character in that essay awoken from sleep as if by "Rilke's armies of reality," "woken by a nameless yearning, a feeling which if followed to its naked conclusion could change [his] life" [...], but who "[…] avoided a self-confrontation." Unlike the character, I wholeheartedly engaged in the necessary emotionally painful self-confrontation.

Lately, I often feel sad it took this long for my self-transformation to occur. Perhaps it was meant to be so. What is not at all sad is this: I am now truly alive for the first time in my life. The adage, an unexamined life is not worth living is one of the seemingly simple but profound thoughts there is. That I am a transformed man I cannot repeat enough. Devotion to the moral, to Truth, to Justice, to Knowledge, to Love, to brotherly love, all these have become my sole concern at this point in my life. I feel I have redeemed my life now that I am exercising my newfound conscience. I feel light, as the gravity of my life up to now has been lifted off my being. I am enjoying a wellness of being, a lightening of the spirit. I feel good about myself. My spirit is enlivened. It is the first time in my life that I feel fulfilled. And, these days I am almost driven to lunacy when I think about the senseless executions, jailing and harassments that philosophic men have suffered under my leadership. So regretful I am now. Whereas we should celebrate and utilize the best of their ideas for the development of Gidaland, for the wellbeing of our people, we plot and wrongly convict them of crimes. We hang them, we shoot them, we poison them, we bomb them, we jail them . . . If only I had been and thought the way I do now, no doubt I would have ruled justly and strived to help Gidaland realize its God-given potentials. I would have labored to revolutionize its jungle existence, create a truly civil society where our people can endeavor to realize their God-given potential. So, my self-imposed task for the rest of my life is to steadfastly struggle to institute in Gidaland a society grounded on morality, justice and freedom for all our people, both in principle and practice. If need be, I will die struggling to realize it!

Everything I have written about Gidaland regarding its jungle existence, and how we, its political leaders, treat it as a for-profit entity; how we unjustly persecute and silence our philosophic men, is not limited to Gidaland. You must comprehend that Gidaland is a prototype of all of our African countries; a particular case that accurately depicts the woeful situation of Africa today. No wonder we, political leaders in Africa, live lavishly while the majority of our people languish in poverty. No wonder many of our people have emigrated, scattered all over the world, human seeds seeking fertile lands, while those who remain are starving body and spirit. Our inculcation of fear has systematically undermined their spirit. (But that will soon change!) They have resorted to using churches and mosques as spiritual refuge from their miserable daily lives . . . As I have in disguise done many times, in wandering our streets, or going to our marketplaces, you will see them, our people. Their lackluster eyes looking about nervously, staring into space, their cheeks sunken, cheekbones overly emphasized. Fear and hunger have achieved what we want of them: to be politically irrelevant masses. Too weak to agitate for social change, too weak to think deeply, totally preoccupied with eking out their meager living, perpetually improvising to make up for all sorts of deficiencies in their material needs, they have become dormant, virtually non-existing members of our society. They have become wasted human resources, potential harbingers of our society's transformation whose energy is being sapped. What devilish objective intellectual, material and spiritual deprivation cannot achieve? What devilish objective the inculcation of fear cannot achieve? Such devilish injustice . . . You should see me now, fuming with such heated rage not even cognac can placate. . . .

Ah! . . . Enough said.

In this essay I have discussed the agonizing human condition in Gidaland, a prototype of all of African countries. I have argued that intellectuals all over the world—betraying their misguided, simplistic understanding of world affairs—have grossly misunderstood its cause. Their simplistic interpretation of Gidaland's plight, of Africa's plight, has resulted in their espousing erroneous recommendations and policies for transforming it. I have, therefore, argued for a mature understanding of it, which should be a philosophical one, as that would most enable a comprehension of it. That is what I have attempted in this essay. It is my hope it will spur further thought and critical debates.

If when you finish reading this essay you deem it nonsensical, naïve, abstract or idealistic, that would reveal a lack of knowledge of human beings and their existence, an inability to think about human beings in a fundamental way. The questions I would then ask of you are these: What essentially is a human being? How essentially is a society created? What makes a society endure? If you thoroughly engage these fundamental questions, you will begin to appreciate the basis of my thoughts, the central idea pulsing in this essay.

I would like to conclude with this statement:

I say this to thinking persons all over the world: the age of innocence, ignorance and apathy is over. You must strive to expose the lies of History. The time has long been overdue you realize that Gidaland today, Africa today, is a jungle brought into being by her historical experience: the agonizing drama of her existence since she was "discovered" by the outside world. I appeal to you all to be profound in your thinking; to be mindful of not letting your God-given ability for reasoning be influenced by conventional thoughts; to not give credence to popular thoughts and modes of thinking; to be brave and leave no stone unturned as you labor to uncover the deeply hidden truth about Existence. I appeal to you all to not be conventional thinkers whose thoughts are hastily baked and charmingly served on the plate of conventional popular opinions.

And I say this to leaders all over the world, whether military or civilian, whether out-rightly despotic or under the guise of "democracy": We are deluding ourselves if we think our domination of Man's life is cemented. The resiliency that characterizes the human spirit will frustrate our demonic ambition; its elasticity is infinitely extendable and will triumph in the end. Tomorrow is always to come. And with the coming of tomorrow comes hope. Man is mortal; Hope is not. . . .

And I say this to leaders in Africa specifically: Enough! Enough! Enough! It is time we dissent. We know Africa is on the violent stage of History, on which is unfolding a bloody drama of Existence. We know we are principal actors in its continuation. We must bravely struggle to stop it. Yes, it is a daunting task but we must bravely confront it. We must effect Africa's emancipation, progress and glory. After much deliberation, this is what I know: The Salvational work will have to start in thought about Existence, leading to this knowledge:

A people is the indigenous Story it tells itself about Existence; its indigenous worldview is that Story.

A people's indigenous worldview is a psychological armor enabling it to engage Existence.

A people's indigenous worldview is the cultural wellspring out of which it derives, and which informs, influences and orders, its way of life.

A people's indigenous worldview and way of life is to it what the root is to the tree: a lifeline. Africans became a tree without its root when their indigenous worldviews and ways of life were supplanted. We all know what happens to a tree sapped of nutrients from its root.

When a people's indigenous worldview is supplanted what ultimately results is that its indigenous way of life (Everything) falls apart, its society becomes a jungle.

The sure way out of the jungle is to first comprehend it is a jungle, then strive to comprehend how and why it came into being, and comprehend that a new worldview is needed, being mindful that the new worldview must necessarily take into account the old worldview, and make meaningful the ongoing suffering of the majority of our people.

Our philosophic persons—poets, novelists, essayists, playwrights, musicians, painters, sculptors—are, collectively, our Storytellers, our "Mythmakers," our Keepers of the Flame warming our hearts, reminding us of what must not be forgotten: Justice, Freedom, Character, Equality, Togetherness, Unity, Progress, Knowledge, Love, brotherly love . . . They are indispensable to the Cultural Rebirth we so crucially need, which is what I have referred to as the Salvational work needed. It is they who are most receptive to Thought, which they strive, often under daunting circumstances, to convey to us.

We have long been looking elsewhere, running helter-skelter seeking salvation from our problems. I assure you we need not do this because the Salvation we seek elsewhere is right here at home. (I recall this Yorùbá proverb: *Ohun tí à nwá ní Sókótó wà ní àpò sòkòtò*—What we are seeking in a far away land is all along in our pockets.) It is not surprising we are looking elsewhere for Salvation. As Okri writes in his essay, "Redreaming the World":

"The oppressed [...] often think of their victors as their standard of aspiration. Lack of historical confidence leads them into this bifurcation of thinking. They have not as a people learnt how to snatch historical confidence from the most unlikely places, from the fact that they are still here on this planet, inhabiting some sort of space, that they often survived slavery and all manner of outrages, drought, famine, dictatorships, bad governments, bitter wars, mass imprisonments and other permutations of human viciousness [...]."

We must comprehend our Salvation is right here at home. Yes, the Salvational work is a daunting task. But undertake it we must! We must be brave, and strive to achieve it. And to be surely prepared for it we need to realize this is requisite: we ourselves, every one of us, need to effect self-transformation, a spiritual rebirth and without such, we will remain deaf to the Message of our philosophic persons; we will remain oblivious to our role in perpetuating our jungle existence, the devilish role we play in allowing others to divide, conquer and rule us and use us to dominate others, our resources. We will continue to lack vision. Without vision there is no true emancipation and progress. I pray we not perish for lack of vision. That I achieve such a rebirth is testament that all can do it too.

Viva philosophic persons everywhere!
Viva Hope! Viva Africa!
I rest my case. And I thank you so much for reading my thoughts.

General Jéjélayé,
Gidaland

# STORIES

## The Allure of Form

One should make time for reverie, leave one's desk sometimes, stroll about the streets, people-watch. The essay can wait. On a beautiful afternoon as this, albeit sweltering, one ought not to spend the whole day writing. I extinguished the cigarette, drank the remaining of my chilled pinot noir, switched-off the computer, grabbed my Khaki trousers, white cotton shirt and beige "NY" bucket hat from atop the bed and fetched my brown belt and brown Birkenstocks sandals from the closet. I contemplated the stereo awhile, decided to leave it on. (It would be rude to interrupt Sarah Vaughan heaving through a ballad, her voice husky.) I grabbed my keys and stopped in the kitchen to get a bottle of water, frosty, from the foggy refrigerator.

I wandered about the city, clutching the now perspiring bottle of water in one hand and Ben Okri's *Dangerous Love* in the other. My shirt unbuttoned down to just above my navel, the sleeves rolled up above my elbows; my scalp sweaty under my hat; beads of sweat frolicking on my torso, waltzing down my abdomen. People walked about clutching bottles of soft drinks and water, many of them scantily dressed. Bare navels, many bejeweled, stared at the world from under tank tops and muscle shirts. Breasts jiggled, their alluring nipples ogling passersby, quickening our pulses.

Drained by the heat I decided to find a quiet coffee shop to read in while sipping coffee.

I selected a table closest to the window with a clear view of the dramatic streets, ordered a large iced coffee, and turned my attention to the streets. A young woman was gesticulating, her lips moving fast. Her male companion stared at her as she talked. She finished talking and settled into a sullen pose, her arms folded across her chest. She and her companion gazed at each other awhile. He now pursed his lips, and ran the back of his hand slowly down her cheek. A hesitant smile appeared on her face. They embraced. Some passersby smiled at them.

"Excuse me . . . your coffee," the waitress said softly, easing me from the reconciling couple outside. She lifted the cup of coffee off the round wood tray balanced on her palm and gingerly laid it on the table, maintaining eye contact with me, a timid smile cowering at the corners of her lips. "Thank you," I said, smiling. "You're welcome," she said, the smile, now bold, tugging at her lips as she left. Halfway toward the kitchen she subtly turned her head. Our eyes met. Then I gulped a mouthful of the coffee, the ice cubes hugging my top lip, refreshing. I gulped some more, wriggled into a more comfortable position and started flipping the pages of *Dangerous Love*, eager to know how Omovo, the protagonist, was coping with his doomed relationship with the married beautiful Ifeyiwa. It was then they crowded into the coffee shop.

They stood at a table close to mine. "This looks good," said one of them. "Yeah, let's sit here," said another. As they sat one of them, a magazine held under her arm, ogled me and briskly raised her eyebrows at me. She was beautiful, as were the others.

They ordered two New York cheesecakes with strawberry topping, two tiramisus and four iced cappuccinos.

The woman who had eyed me flirtatiously put the magazine on the table. Adorning its glossy chicly designed front cover was a photograph of a muscled and pretty-faced male model. His face had been painstakingly accentuated: thick dark eyebrows trimmed and waxed; eyelashes straightened; high cheekbones outlined; full lips lubricated. His demeanor was erotic: bright dark eyes narrowed; lubricated lips pursed.

"Damn. He's handsome," said the woman who had eyed me. "Handsome?" said the woman who had concurred they sat at that table. "Where others are men, he's a god. Perfect." Another one said, "Check out his eyelashes. He's the man." The fourth woman sat quietly gazing at the model's enticing physique.

Not wanting them to know I was eavesdropping on their conversation, I pretended to read. In my head, thinking about the essay I was working on earlier, *The Allure of Form*, I said to the one who thought the model a god: "Don't you want to know what's in his head?" I was amazed when, as if she had read my thoughts, she said to the others: "With a face and body like his, he doesn't need a brain. What's in his head can't be ridiculously shallow anyhow." Her comment made me wonder whether good looks (Form) signify pith (Content), and reminded me of this:

On a previous afternoon of that summer, I had gone to Central Park to wrap myself in the tranquility of reverie. I sat on a lone wooden bench shaded by a tree and facing a pond on which a family of geese frolicked and pigeons pecked the ground.

A man soon walked over to the bench.

"May I?" He pointed at the space beside me.

"Please," I said.

He sat.

"Nice, right?"

"What?" I said, raising my head from a page of Mario Vargas Llosa's *The War of the End of the World.*

"The park."

"Oh, yes. And this is one of its best areas."

"Yep, a great place to meet women. They like to hang out here." He smiled.

"Not today," I said.

"Your accent, where're you from originally?"

"Buluwayo."

"Bull who? He smiled nervously.

"Buluwayo," I repeated, offering no explanation, enjoying his ignorance. Let him consult a world atlas.

The conversation deepened. He told me he had recently divorced. And described how a popular female pop singer makes him forget "everything" when he sees her music videos. That he religiously sees them whenever they are played on television. "She does something to me that I just can't explain. Her looks . . . her face . . . her body . . . damn . . . she's fine. She really gets me whenever I see her music videos."

"Who is this woman?" I said, frowning at him, thinking he had never met nor conversed with the said singer. He knows her only as a singer whose image inflames him with passion.

Any wonder he was divorced?

He mentioned a name I was not familiar with.

I shrugged.

"You don't know her?"

I shook my head back and forth.

He stared at me, and soon left his place beside me on the bench.

I was glad he left, and turned my attention to the family of geese, happy to catch a baby goose in the act of jumping onto its mother's back, shrieking ecstatically. I smiled at the geese, and started flipping through the pages of *The War of the End of the World*, eager to resume reading that magnificent novel.

My experience with the man in the park had rekindled my interest to write about the power Form exerts on the emotion, which had culminated in the essay.

As I sat eavesdropping and musing on the conversation of the women here was proof of the relevance of my essay, I thought. They were not concerned with the handsome model's content. None of them opined it would be nice to know where he was intellectually; what moved him; what his sources of joy and sorrow were; what his thoughts were about the state of the world, about cultural tolerance and mutual coexistence . . . They, as did the man in the park, had validated this age-old truth (this is the gist of the essay) about the majority of human beings: We adore Form, often in disregard of Content, and let it inform and influence our relationships. Only a minority of us transcends that situation and let Content inform and influence our relationships. It is an existential concern we ought to contemplate (I was arguing in the essay) because when the relationships the majority of us initiate are informed and influenced by Form, our ethical and social life are warped.

Our focus tends to be on the material. Rather than inner life, we venerate and espouse outer life. The repercussion, often, is that we remain discontented where it matters most: psychological contentment. A feeling that something is missing plagues us. And we should not blame ourselves for this because attraction to Form is a trait bequeathed upon us all by Desire, one of the fundamental traits that characterize the human being. Nonetheless, we need not be enslaved to Form. We ought to strive for a new measure of ourselves, endeavor to let Content inform and influence our relationships. (I had tagged a Post-it note to my computer to conclude the essay with this statement:) Here is a point to consider: a form-based relationship is ultimately doomed given that, after the initial giddiness characteristic of romance, it is often ephemeral. Discontentment usually follows. We, therefore, should endeavor to transform our natural attachment to Form. Such a personal transformation is crucial to our self-contentment. It will change our lives as it has the potential to liberate us from all the social conditioning that suppresses rather than frees our spirit.

That was what I meant to argue in the essay, but my experience with one of the women in the coffee shop revolutionized my thought. As I sat there pretending to read, they paid their bill and got ready to leave. As they filed out, my admirer, the one with the magazine, again ogled me. I maintained her gaze, smiling at her, grateful she had not given up on me as I had not responded to her earlier, and invited her to sit with me awhile. "We're leaving," she said, a feeble smile twitching her lips. I pleaded with a puckering of my lips and mouthed "please", maintaining eye contact with her. "I'll meet you guys outside," she said to her friends. They looked at me; then at her, their faces animated in smiles, and crowded out of the coffee shop murmuring. Alone, we played at shyness, conversed and exchanged phone numbers. As we talked, I marveled at her beauty. A sylph she was. With a noble face adorned with high cheekbones; lustrous skin the color of dusk; bright eyes dark as night; full lips like mature crescent moons; teeth like burnished ivory. I knew nothing about her content, and it was at that moment unimportant to me. I was so enchanted by her form. And was intent on calling her that night for a date the next day, perhaps an afternoon spent in Central Park, and dinner at my favorite restaurant in Chinatown.

She strutted out of the coffee shop. At the door, she turned and bade me goodbye with a subtle wave of her right hand raised up to her proud bosom. What a glorious gesture. I waved back. And sat thinking I have just now been charmed by Form, a tendency I often decried, impatient with those so captivated. Acknowledging, finally, that Form is divine, our attraction to it inevitable. And eager to get back home and start rewriting the essay, grateful I had indulged my desire to walk about the city that afternoon.

The waitress avoided eye contact with me as I paid my bill and left the coffee shop.

## The Time Traveler

Now that his moment of departure is imminent I hover above him watching him. . . .

As I am presently no longer in him, his spirit devoid, emaciated flesh lay motionless on the bed. He is breathing intermittently, his eyes closed. . . . I remember well our beginning together some seven hundred moons ago when we were about to embark on the journey here to the world of mortals. I remember the moment he knelt in front of Olódùmarè, the Creator, to receive his destiny. Upon receiving his destiny we started on our way here.

We arrived at the Gate, where we encountered Onîbodè, the Keeper of the Gate, to whom any being coming into the world must answer some questions before passing through.

"Where are you going?" Onîbodè asked him.

"I am going to earth," he said.

"What are you going to do there?"

"I will be born a Yorùbá, to a man named Olúdòtun Ransome-Kútì, and his wife, Olúfúnmiláyò Thomas Ransome-Kútì, in a town named Abéòkúta, in the righteous land named Africa, whose destiny is being altered for the worse, whose godly nature is being devoured by Evil. It is the human incarnates of Evil, and their human supporters that I will spend my life there battling. . . ."

"I will be born twice. The first time I will die in infancy because my parents will name me Heidegger, after a German missionary acquaintance of theirs. I will be greatly offended by this, and will revolt against it by departing earth soon after that. I will return there through the same parents, and this time they will give me the befitting name: Olúfelá Olúségun Olúdòtun Ransome-Kútì. . . ."

"I will display my uncompromising character and sense of earthly mission early in life by being a stubborn child who questions everything. My parents, especially my mother, will whip me a lot for it. Regardless of this I will be very close to my mother. She will be my best friend and steadfast ally. . . ."

"I will grow up to bear the cross of my people's miserable existence, the soldier for the downtrodden, fighting for them their righteous battle. My music will be my formidable weapon. I will suffer greatly for my effort. My struggle—my destined labor of love for Justice, for Freedom, for Love—will not bear fruit until much later in the future. . . ."

"For some time I will be somewhat ignorant, overlook my destiny, overly indulge in the frivolities of earthly life, devote my vibrant energy to seeking egoistic recognition, and material riches. . . ."

"Around the time of my three hundred and seventieth moons on earth I will journey to America where I will meet a woman. It is she who will redeem me from all that unnecessary foolishness. She will renew me with her love and knowledge. My chance encounter with her will remind me of my destiny, and will better prepare me to fulfill it. I will return home a renewed man and will thenceforth dedicate myself wholeheartedly to fulfilling my destiny. . . ."

"Many of my people will ignore me in my struggle for their freedom and wellbeing. They will call me a 'troublemaker', 'ruffian', 'hemp-smoker', and all sorts of names. This is the cross of my kind: to be abused, misunderstood, ridiculed by the same people whose liberation and progress he is laboring to realize for them. My succor will be Woman—of whom I will have many; my queens, my psychic and physical backbone—and Music and Humor and Laughter and Hemp, lots of hemp. . . ."

"On the day of my seven hundred and five and one half moons on earth I will draw my final breath. I will be honored with a big funeral and much fanfare. My departure from earth will cause grief for many; even those who were my foes will grieve privately."

"You have spoken your destiny. It is sealed!" Oníbodè said.

And that was exactly what happened when we got here. He departed soon after he was born the first time, as he hated his given name, Heidegger. "I want a Yorùbá name!" his soul cried out then. He stayed the second time, this time that is now ending, having been named Olúfelá, the short form of which is Felá.

Not long after he returned from America there was this moment: He was alone. He stood in front of a mirror, staring at himself. After he had been doing that for a while, he started to soliloquize: "I have seen the Light again. I now recall who I am, my destiny. My path is clear to me now. I must be true to my destiny … I must carry the Cross stoically, wail the message incessantly, in all pitches, bright, dark, robust, even jarring and irritating. I must wake up my people. I must open their eyes. I must light up the dull bulb of knowledge in their heads." As he said these words his eyes became noticeably radiant, as they usually are in immortals living in the flesh. He remained staring at himself in the mirror, then took a long drag on his fatly rolled hemp, held his breath for a while, exhaled, slowly, the smoke undulating in front of his intent eyes, hugging his face. "Africa, I will fight for you as I am meant to," he said.

And since then he has been true to his destiny, wailing loudly, reminding you mortals that you have strayed from the way; the way of righteousness that Olódùmarè meant for you to live by. Cautioning you that there are among you wolves in sheep's clothing whose existence and evil deeds are impossible without the support of many of you.

Presently: He remains motionless on the bed, gasping intermittently, his eyes still closed. Yes, his departure is imminent, but when he is gone do not think of him as dead. It is his flesh that will be no more. His spirit, for which his flesh is merely the bodily vessel, lives. As will live on for all time the message he has been wailing through his music all these moons he has been here. The immortality, the permanent essence of his message, made audible and thus tangible in his music, is what he meant to convey by changing the first half of his family name, Ransome, to Aníkúlápó—possessor of (possessing) control over death. With Aníkúlápó he expresses his fearlessness, and his immortality, not him the person, but that which he personifies, the message for which he is a conduit and here to wail. This does not, however, exclude the immortality of his person because divine messages are immortal and the person through whose voice they are promulgated and thus made real and enduring, is deathless. Thus the immortality of the message inevitably confers on the messenger as well.

Much has been said about him. Many of you mortals have called him "arrogant", "radical", "nuisance", "agitator", "hooligan", "reckless." However, many of you, his friends and foes alike, concur that he is a gifted artist, innovative, and fearless, undaunted by the cruelty he repeatedly suffered. What many of you do not know about him is his essence: a spirit being camouflaging as a philosopher, a teacher, a historian, a social critic, a humorist for whom Music, a gift of which Olódùmarè gave him, is merely a medium through which to fulfill his destiny, to wail the gospel of Redemption. . . .

And, yes, through his music he fulfilled his destiny, wailing, all these moons, for the realization of Justice, Freedom, Love, brotherly love, Unity, Togetherness, Character, Courage here in your world, and the restoration of your indigenous culture as the machinery needed to restore your Mother, and all of you Her children, to Her erstwhile righteous way; the machinery needed to lift Her out of the black hole of an existence in which she and all of you have been sunk. These constitute the essence of his message. He wailed them throughout his music. Listen with your Heart, please, to his effort to erase fear and apathy from your minds in his song "Fear Not for Man"; his lamentation of the miserable existence plaguing the majority of you today in "Original Sufferhead"; his poignant commentary on your neglect of your indigenous culture in "Upside Down"; his effort to caution you against conventional education in "Mr. Follow Follow"; his howling at the corrupt practices of many of your leaders in "Army Arrangement," "International Thief Thief," and "Underground System"; his denunciation of the blatant abuse of your human rights in "Sorrow Tears and Blood"; his call for your psychological emancipation in "Colonial Mentality"; his adoration of your Mother and composition for Her wellbeing in "Africa-Center of the World"; his self-explained composition "Music Against Second Slavery" . . . Listen with your heart, please, to these and many others of his songs. . . .

Surely, you mortals know that your world is misguided

and misled, plagued with evil. Domination—in numerous mind boggling, spirit unsettling guises and disguises—not Love rules and guides your world, Money not Love lords over you. You know, ought to know, that calamity of annihilating capacity; of apocalyptic magnitude is lurking amidst you, covertly unleashing terror on you. . . .

Presently: He is staring at the ceiling where a colorful scene has now appeared, his eyes wide open, a gentle smile lightly tugging at the corners of his dry, emaciated lips … He continues to stare at the ceiling. In the scene his mother—regal in a white Yorùbá garb of ìró and bùbá, with a matching gèlè crowning her head—is smiling blissfully at him. Behind her an orchestra is playing a divine tune. She is waving at him; a gesture for him to come to her. Yes, he loved his mother. She was his best friend, his mightiest alátìléyìn (existential anchor) as he had labored to fulfill his destiny all these moons. Her untimely departure from this life over two hundred moons ago left him feeling vulnerable and lonely, caused him great mental and emotional anguish from which he never fully recovered. So, now seeing his mother smiling and waving at him he is a pleasantly surprised and joyous son . . . He is now smiling at his mother, attempting to move his lips as if to say something to her . . . His eyes are fixed on her, the smile on his face still gently tugging at his lips . . . He exhales now . . . He is still. . . .

This was not his first appearance in your world. He was here before many, many moons ago in the land you call Egypt today, where he was then called Amen Ra Heru Kuti. As in that time cycle I have relished being his Orí—"personality soul" or "guardian Angel," as many of you call me—during all these moons he has lived here in your world wailing the message, your Mother's and yours' Tears and Laughter. He will be back again and again until the message becomes a reality here.

## Farewell Ceremony

In our culture, a farewell ceremony is organized when a person is to travel to a foreign country for an extended period of time. The purpose of the ceremony is to commemorate the imminent departure of the traveler from the society and to pray for her or his safe journey and return.

There are two types of the ceremony: the indigenous, traditional, and the foreign, modern.

The traditional ceremony is prevalent among our older generation. A prophet conducts it in the traditional manner; guests wear traditional clothing; they are fed traditional food and drinks. The modern ceremony is popular among our younger generation. It does not involve a prophet conducting it nor a formal prayer. Friends and neighbors, dressed in shabby tee-shirts, short and long sleeve shirts and trousers and blouses and skirts, congregate to celebrate the good fortunes of the departing person. ("Good fortunes" because it was and still is deemed "prestigious" to travel to Europe or North America for schooling, and more so if, as was true of me, America is the destination.) They eat homemade foreign food including foreign styled cakes. They drink Coca Cola, Pepsi, Seven Up, Fanta, beer, Guinness. They dance to American pop music. They flirt with one another.

No formal invitation is needed to farewell ceremonies; everyone comes.

Mama planned a traditional farewell ceremony for me. She invited the prophet in our neighborhood—a skinny man with graying hair, perpetually reddish eyes and yellow teeth—to oversee the ceremony. The prophet is the cultural heart of our society, its spiritual custodian. The prophet conducts indigenous healing ceremonies, foretells the future, interprets dreams, serves as the link between the spiritual and the temporal. . . .

On the day of my ceremony, the prophet, who had arrived early and eaten, took his place on Mama's enormous mat that we used for the ceremony in the backyard of our rooming house. The sitting arrangement was concentric. In the core sat the prophet, Mama and me. I sat directly in front of the prophet. Mama sat beside me to my right. On the mat in front of the prophet was a bottle of ògógóró, our local gin, and several kolanuts on a plate. In the outer circle surrounding us sat the guests, our fellow tenants and their children and others from the neighborhood. I scanned the crowd. There was Mrs. Sadé; our neighbor and through whom I got my job, uncle Súlè; an unemployed man in our neighborhood to whom I give some money now and then, Jimoh; my friend the painter, Foláké; my co-worker and lover, Sarah; a beautiful young woman from our neighborhood, Conny; another local beauty. . . .

Some people chatting animatedly, others congratulating me for my "good fortune". . . .

The prophet loudly cleared his throat. The crowd responded with numerous "shhhhhh." Silence descended on the gathering.

The prophet again cleared his throat, gently this time. "My people, let us begin," he said. "We gather here today to pray for our departing son, Òdodo, who will leave us to go to America for his education." He smiled as he said "America."

The prophet placed his forefinger on my forehead.

"The chicken must come home to roost, not so?" he said gazing at the crowd.

"It is so!" the crowd responded collectively.

"Just as the chicken must come home to roost," the prophet said staring at me, his eyes fiery, "so you, Òdodo, shall come back home to us!"

"Àse!" the crowd responded collectively.

"You will never be one of those who go to foreign lands and forget their homeland, forsake their ancestral ways, refuse to return here to the land of your ancestors!"

"Àse!" the crowd responded collectively.

"You will succeed in all your endeavors!"

"Àse!" the crowd responded collectively.

"Your paths shall be clear to you!"

"Àse!"

"All the days of your life, you will never want!"

"Àse!"

"You will not want in America!"

"Àse!"

"Ògún, our god of iron, will fight your battles for you.

"Àse!"

Ògún will be before you and after you.

"Àse!"

Ògún will guide you in your every move everyday of your life!"

"Àse!"

"You will not be a victim of gunshot in America."

"Àse!"

"The bullet will be your enemy and will flee from you!"

"Àse!"

"All I have prayed for will be answered! Olódùmarè, our heavenly Father, the Creator of the Universe and all that dwells in It, has listened."

"Àse!"

The prophet paused, thrice poured some ògógóró on the floor, drank some straight from the bottle, noisily rinsed his mouth with it and swallowed.

"Òdodo," the prophet called my name, staring at me, "who is this woman?" He pointed to Mama.

"My mother," I said.

"You all heard that?" He gazed at the crowd. "Òdodo said this woman seated beside him is his mother."

"We heard," the crowd responded collectively.

"Bùnmi," he gazed at Mama, "your son has identified you as his mother. You are the one who brought him into this world. You fed him milk from your breast. You catered to him when he was a helpless little child until now, not so?"

"It is so," responded Mama and the crowd collectively.

"Should a child forget his mother?"

"No!" the crowd responded collectively.

"A child does not disrespect or neglect his mother, not so?"

"It is so!"

"Honor your father and your mother is the rule of conduct taught to us by our ancestors. Not so?"

"It is so!"

"Òdodo you will honor your mother!"

"Àse!"

"Now that you are going to America, you will not neglect her!"

"Àse!"

"You will not forget her!"

"Àse!"

"Olódùmarè will give you the means to do your duty to her!"

"Àse!"

"You will always remember her!"

"Àse!"

"You will do right by her!"

"Àse!"

"In America, you will not be influenced by bad ways. You will not mingle with people of bad character!"

"Àse!"

"You will bring glory back to our people!"

"Àse!"

"All I have prayed will be answered! Olódùmarè, our heavenly Father, the Creator of the Universe and all that dwells in It, has listened."

"Àse!"

The prophet paused, thrice poured some ògógóró on the floor, drank some straight from the bottle, rinsed his mouth with it, swallowed . . .

As the ceremony progressed I was only half listening for I was thinking about the call and response manner of the prayer. It reminded me of the same in the jazz music I had heard in Jimoh's studio.

While the ceremony continued I let my eyes wander over the crowd. With big wooden spoons, some women stirred in huge pots steaming over makeshift stoves energized by firewood. Mouth watering aroma filled the air. Mama dabbed the corner of her damp eyes with the edge of her wrapper. Foláké gazed at me. I smiled at her. She smiled back, feebly, a solemn look on her face. Many of the young women batted their eyes at me. Many of the mothers rocked their irritated infants, pacified them with milk from their gorged breasts. Many of the older men sat with their palms on their cheeks. Jimoh winked at me. I smiled at him. Uncle Súlè smiled at me. I smiled back. Then, Mama elbowed me and, as if nothing had happened, quickly looked ahead of her. A sharp pain shot through my side; such strength from a smallish woman, I thought. . . .

To avoid the appearance of inattention, thus ensuring I do not get another elbow attack from Mama, I focused my eyes on the ground in front of me. I embarked on a mental journey to America, thinking about my arriving there and getting immersed in Development Studies . . . Thinking about our people, our dire existence. We are abundantly provided for by nature; we are rich in raw and mineral resources; we are rich in human resources—all the jobless university graduates aimlessly roaming the streets, holes in the soles of their shoes, their faces gaunt from hunger—yet poverty abounds in our society. Why is that so? Yes, there is General Jéjélayé. Is he to blame for our problems? Undoubtedly. But is it not possible that what we need are more of us young people arming ourselves with Knowledge, and using it to undermine the domination of our life by the General and his cronies, using it to transform our life? . . . Why are African countries poor while the countries of Western Europe and North America, less rich in raw and mineral resources compared to Africa, are prosperous? Am I naive in thinking Knowledge is power? Is our miserable existence fossilized, beyond the possibility of transformation? Is Hope an illusion? . . . I sat there on the mat thinking about all these things, the crowd passionately bellowing 'Àse' in unison.

I concluded as I usually did: to comprehend the miserable existence in Gidaland, in Africa, formal education in the social sciences is pivotal. Why? I believe in an increasingly interdependent world, we, the young people in Gidaland, in Africa, The Beautyful Ones Who Are Now Born, must thoroughly understand how the world works in order to achieve a transformation in our own society. We are the future. I will do my part. It is the only reason for my decision to embark upon graduate education in Development Studies. I firmly believe a deeper understanding of human beings, of how to mobilize them to achieve social change, would be the way to a better tomorrow for our people, for Africa.

"All I have prayed for Olódùmarè has listened to and will answer. May Olódùmarè continue to grant our prayers," the prophet said, concluding the prayer.

In response to the last call of prayer by the prophet, the crowd bellowed a louder, more forceful and drawn-out final response: "Àààà-seeee!"

The prophet thrice poured some ògógóró on the floor, drank some straight from the bottle and handed the bottle to Mama. She drank a little and passed it to me. I drank a little and passed it along. In that manner everyone drank some of the ògógóró. The prophet then halved one kolanut into two lobes, took one lobe, placed the other on the plate with the rest of the kolanuts, and passed the plate to Mama. He bit a piece of his lobe and chewed vigorously. Mama bit a piece of the lobe left on the plate by the prophet, put the rest back on the plate and passed it to me. I bit a small piece of that same lobe and passed the plate on. In this manner we all ate a bit of kolanut.

The communal sharing of ògógóró and kolanut ended the prayer part of the ceremony. Shortly after, Mama, assisted by the women, served everyone—the prophet first, then the elderly, and then everyone else—white rice and fried yellow plantain garnished with marinated goat meat cooked in well-seasoned tomato sauce, and palm wine and soft drinks. Here, it seems our soft drinks contain a high level of gas. (Perhaps inflating our empty stomach is a merciful method devised by the beverage industry to satiate our hunger.) People belched loudly now and then. You would have thought a belching contest was in progress. After the meal, people started milling about, chatting animatedly, intermittently sucking on their teeth and digging into them. Some did this with toothpicks, others with their nails, still others with the sharp tips of knives in an effort to hunt the pieces of meat hiding there.

Later, in accordance with our culture, as the crowd departed, the adults stopped to briefly chat with Mama and hand her whatever cash gifts they could afford, money that helped pay for the expense of the ceremony.

The next day Mama and me journeyed to Boyo village to see my grandparents. On the night of our last day with them, we all assembled at our ancestral shrine in the courtyard of their house. Under the calm gaze of the pregnant moon my grandfather sacrificed a rooster, and summoned and besieged Ògún, my deity, with pleas to accompany me on my journey across the great sea to New York City, to protect me there always, and to safely bring me back to them.

Later that night, my grandfather took me to visit the chief of the village, the Moses of the village who has for some five decades guided our people living there. My grandfather had been taking me to visit him since I was a youngster. The chief welcomed us warmly and asked us to sit with him on a big palm leaf mat spread on the ground in his courtyard. His wife brought us a keg of palm wine and poured us a calabash each, first serving the chief, then my grandfather and then me. The chief then offered us kolanut, and, gazing at me, commented on how much I had grown. He and my grandfather exchanged a certain look. My grandfather told him of my impending journey to America for schooling. They again exchanged that certain look. As they chitchatted, the chief glanced at me from time to time. Before we left, pressing his forefinger onto the center of my forehead, the chief besieged our ancestors with prayer for my journey across the sea to be safe, that they look after me while I am in America and bring me back home safely body and spirit.

After supper that night, while Mama and my grandmother were in the house conversing, I was in the courtyard spending time with my grandfather. He told me he will continue to pray for me, and offer sacrifices to our ancestors so that a certain prophecy about me may be deflected. And that he will continue to pray for me and offer sacrifices so that if the prophecy must be, that I have the strength and wherewithal to fulfill it. I did not understand what he meant and he refused to expound on it. He told me not to tell Mama he said that to me. He will tell her himself when the time is right to do so.

Early the next morning Mama and me returned to the city. That evening Foláké came to see me. Although I had told Mama about her, it was the first time they met in person. She wished me well in New York City and commented she is sure I will not forget home. "Of course, not," I said. Later, outside, waiting for a taxi to take her home, "Òdodo, I want you to know that I love you very much," she said. "I do to too," I said. We embraced. I thanked her for her love and support, and promised to write her.

A week later I left home for distant New York City. Mama went with me to the airport. Under ideal conditions the airport is about one hour of driving from my neighborhood. But because of our infamous traffic jams, it is often impossible to get there in that time. So we left home hours early so as to assure that I did not miss my early morning flight. I hired a taxi for the trip. Through a gash in the floor of the vehicle, where the steel had rusted and left a hole, I saw the bare road beneath as it grunted along. This is typical of many of the taxis and buses that populate our roads.

"Send me a post card from there to let me know you arrived safely . . . you know I will worry if I do not hear from you," Mama said. We were inside the check-in terminal at the airport. Mama was referring to Amsterdam, my transit city en route to New York City.

"Yes, Mama . . . Mama, do not worry, I will be fine," I said, held her hand. Her eyes were damp. With her other hand, she grabbed the edge of her wrapper and dabbed the corners of her eyes. "Mama, please do not cry," I said wiping her tears with my fingertips.

I had only carry-on luggage, so when my flight was announced for check-in, I got ready to proceed to the "passenger only" terminal for customs and immigration clearance. I prostrated full length on the floor of the airport in front of Mama bidding her goodbye. She embraced me when I got up, held on to me, her heart drumming a fast tempo on my chest. She reluctantly released her firm hold of me. And traced my face with the tip of her middlefinger, underneath my eyes, down to the tip of my nose, the rim of my nostrils, my cheekbones, my chin and held my cheek in her palm, all the while staring into my eyes. Then she turned and walked away from me. I stood watching her walk towards the exit. As she neared it, she stopped, turned and gazed at me. I noticed her lips were moving, indicating she was whispering something. Then, she spat on her palm and rubbed it on her head, turned and walked out of the airport without looking back. I knew the taxi driver who drove us to the airport was waiting for her outside. I had paid him to drive her back home. I hoisted my mostly books filled bag onto my shoulder—-the weight shot a pain through my arm—-and trudged along to the immigration and customs terminal. . . .

Having gone through immigration and customs inspections, I proceeded to the departure lounge. I sat at a far corner of the lounge awaiting the boarding announcement for my flight.

Then nostalgia gripped me.

I became overwhelmed with mixed feelings about leaving home. But the journey had to be made. To become an adult requires the child leave home and the sanctuary it provides. An individual does not see himself or herself but by his or her reflection in a mirror: an individual must step outside of himself or herself to objectively understand himself or herself. Gidaland and the other countries in Africa are not entities unto themselves. They exist in an interdependent global community of nations and function economically, politically and socially within it. Thus, if I am to meaningfully understand Gidaland, Africa, I reminded myself, I must contemplate her from afar. Later that morning I departed for Amsterdam en route to New York City. It would be years before I again set foot in Gidaland.

. . .

## The Black hole Days

The fall semester began on the fourth week of my arrival in New York City. Another stage in the journey of life began for me. I had no idea a black hole lurked ahead of me, my fall into it inevitable.

I had begun graduate school as a doctoral student in Development Studies full of zeal to attain knowledge on developing a society. Alas, how was I to have known for my journey to Knowledge I had chosen a deceptive guide and path?

Myself, I understand fairly well and can manage. I am a resolute person with a steadfast sense of calling to labor for the progress of Gidaland, my country; labor for the progress of Africa, my continent; labor for the wellbeing of our people; and blessed with the financial support of an anonymous English woman resident in London, Mrs. Piety, financing my graduate education, which she believed God ordained. But some things are beyond one's control. I had no idea I would become so dejected to the point of attempting to do what I did one winter during that period of my black hole of an existence. . . .

Besides being exceptionally cold, bleak that winter was. Blues everywhere you looked. Thick clouds blanketed the sky refusing to let the sun smile on the city and enliven it. The climate was numbing. Trees had withered; their sapped limbs endured relentless thrashing by the ferocious wind; their groaning cry a mournful melody in the air. The streets of Manhattan were mostly deserted. People, it seemed, rarely went out except to work. You see them—forlorn-looking, tight-lipped—mostly during the early morning and evening rush-hours confronting the frigid weather, their grim faces poking above their bulky long winter coats. . . .

It was a miserable period in my life. What was to be my second year in graduate school was about to begin. But I was not among the students who thronged to the school to register for classes, and who, when classes started, crowded the theatre-like lecture halls. I had become disillusioned with academic social sciences and decided to sever my intellectual, quasi-religious attachment to it; had decided to desert it as my guide and path to Knowledge. My textbooks and "recommended readings" I had abandoned in my bookcase where they sat coated with dust. I incessantly recalled my conversation with Mika, my flower, in Amsterdam, where I met her en route to New York City. She had said: "Dear, don't look to academia for knowledge. Don't rely on modern social sciences. If you do, dear, you'll be greatly disappointed." . . .

If only I had known she was right, of course I would not have entrusted my intellectual heart to academia, saved myself from this agony.

Some time around the last semester of my first year in graduate school I began to have doubts about the relevance of Development Studies in imparting to its students the knowledge crucial to achieving societal development. Imagine that. I had chosen Development Studies as my focus precisely for the purpose of acquiring that knowledge, ignoring Mama's passionate plea that I study Business Administration. My choice had greatly annoyed her. But that had not stopped me from remaining adamant about my choice. Her teary eyes regarding me, I had assured her I would do my duty to her: ensure her wellbeing, as a son must to his mother. I had grieved over causing much pain to the woman so dear to me. And had voluntarily journeyed across the historic Atlantic Ocean to be right there in New York City with the sole aim of mastering the nuts and bolts of how Gidaland could achieve development, surmount the misery plaguing our people. And there I was in New York City having doubts about Development Studies, which I had passionately believed would impart to me the knowledge needed to transform my society. . . .

There I was in New York City seeing places, meeting people, experiencing America's psychical and social reality. There I was struggling with the maddening task of comprehending it all; the maddening task of comparing and contrasting it with that of my native Gidaland; thoughts mushrooming in my head, threatening to burst through my earlobes, nostrils, eyes; driving myself to the verge of insanity. And surviving that intellectual ordeal, a labor of love for Knowledge I happily endured, giddy with joy, and begun to comprehend that in New York City, in rich and democratic America, are extant the miserable existence I had erroneously thought was unique to poor and dictatorial Gidaland. Begun to comprehend that, yes, there was poverty in America, there was domination in clever guises and disguises, there was a feeling of helplessness and spiritual anxiety among many, poor and rich alike. That made me realize social organization is a Herculean task. Made me realize the issue of the development of a society, so dear to my heart, cannot be reduced to a listing of requisite measures, a handy enumeration of the "nuts and bolts" for achieving development, as conventional social scientists assert, teaching me (its students) lies, half-truths, manufactured truths, lecturing it into my head in the classroom; in books, journals, newspapers; on the radio. . . .

What I had seen of the impoverished condition of sections of New York City showed me a side of America we do not see in Gidaland, in Africa. It made me realize America is far from being a perfect society, which makes sense because social organization is a most complex affair, and no society can be perfect because perfection belongs, can only be, in the realm of God. However, I found this troubling, revealing: that sections of New York City are impoverished proves a country need not be underdeveloped, ruled by a dictator to exist in poverty. Therefore, dictatorship itself is not the real cause of the dire existence—or underdevelopment, to use the parlance of academic social sciences—of Gidaland, of Africa. I came to realize this about academic social sciences: They do not understand Africa at all; they are in fact not really interested in a profound understanding of that enigma called human being; they are inept in the pursuit of knowledge about social existence. . . .

So it was that academic social sciences shattered my hope in it as a knowledgeable and dependable guide in my quest for knowledge about developing a society, bettering the life of its people. This quest had brought me to the door of one of the "finest" institutions of higher learning in the United States; one of the most prestigious institutions of higher learning in the world.

And so it was I lost interest in life and living. I became

lax with the body hygiene Mama had meticulously inculcated in me since I was a youngster. I let grow a kinky beard I did not bother to neaten and which grew into a dark jungle, an outward manifestation of my inner confusion, and I did not bother to shower for days at a time. And I started to smoke, initially a few cigarettes a day, and eventually I chain smoked. Having become a smoker I understood the seemingly idiotic comment Abdul, my dear friend and future publisher, once made to me about the enchanting power of the spirit of tobacco. My desire to be so enchanted so as to not think about my depression was why I decided to smoke. Initially I smoked intermittently; soon I smoked constantly. So bewitched I was by the spirit of tobacco. And I started to drink. I am not talking about drinking an occasional bottle of beer like I used to. I became a connoisseur of "*vin ordinaire*," and "*vin de pays*" several glasses of which I daily drank.

How did my passionate relationship with red wine start? I was as usual out walking about my neighborhood one day. On my way back to my apartment I decided on impulse to stop at "Master Cheng's Wines & Spirits." I inquired of Master Cheng, the proprietor, which wine to get. "Red or White?" he said. "Red, I guess," I said. "Okay. The question is really about what to look for in a red wine. So, what do you think one should look for in a red wine?" he said, gazing at me like a tutor challenging his pupil with a question. I shrugged. "Think," he said. "I really do not know," I said. "Okay, okay, Master Cheng will tell you." He proceeded to lecture me on the subject. "What do you look for in a red wine? . . . you look for whether it is made of one type of grape . . . Cabernet Sauvignon, Syrah, Merlot . . . or a mixture of any two, or all of them together . . . you look for the date it is bottled . . . some Merlot are best drunk young, others older . . . you look for whether it is bottled on the producing estate. These are three useful ways to know whether the wine will taste good. People think it is the price but that is not necessarily the case. There are many good red wines, well rounded, smooth taste, that are not that expensive. Trust me, Master Cheng does not lie." He smiled.

Master Cheng walked to a table at a corner of the

store on which sat breathing bottles of red wine, several gaping goblets attending them. He poured from one of the bottles into a goblet. "Try this," he said, and handed me the drink. He stood gazing at me as I drank. The wine tasted good, but sharp, vinegary, a bit like a fruit not sun-ripened. "Now, try this one," he handed me another. Nice taste, smooth, a bit vinegary but not as sharp as the previous one. "And this." It tasted good, with a hint of bitterness, and somewhat heavy, with particles in it, as if one is drinking the dreg of palm wine, which I sometimes drank back in Gidaland. "And now, try this one," he said, smiling as he handed me the goblet, as if he knew I would be most excited by the taste of this one. And I was. It tasted smooth, non-vinegary, and intensely fruity. The smile on my face betrayed my excitement. "I knew that you would like it. It is a Merlot. The one before is a Syrah, unfiltered. The one before that is a mixture of all three grapes. And the first one is a young Cabernet Sauvignon.

After Master Cheng's lecture I soon became adept at recognizing thrifty, gracious Merlot. I would spot her sitting boldly among her aristocratic neighbors. And thus I became her devoted lover, always giddy from the heady smell of her, the feel of her between my teeth, on my gum, palate, tongue, throat, and the heady warm feeling down my throat as I swallow her. Initially I indulged in her moderately. Gradually, intense my desire for her became. I daily romanced her, five, six times a day, and still itched for more. . . .

The whole of that winter I nestled in the warmth of my apartment, and dedicated my days to romancing Merlot, my devoted lover, dependable succor for my emotional pain, and chain smoking cigarettes, smoking myself to oblivion. I rarely left my apartment. When I did, it was for three reasons: To go have dinner, my only meal for the day, at a Senegalese restaurant I liked. I always ordered the same food, *Debe,* well seasoned grilled lamb steaks served on a bed of fluffy white rice and garnished with thinly sliced caramelized onion (sweet as honey!) cooked in curry sauce, and cubes of fried yellow plantains. Or to go to a tobacco shop in my neighborhood to buy more cigarettes or to Master Cheng's to buy more wine. . . .

I became indifferent to the wellbeing of Gidaland, of Africa. Africa was regressing not progressing. Her houses were further falling apart. Corruption and illicit creation of wealth continued to undermine her livelihood. The twin beasts of inflation and hunger continued to torment her: the one gnawing at her, the other slowly devouring her. The powers of the world continued to molest her for their own gain, cunningly dividing and conquering her children as they always have. I heard about all this on news from BBC, Radio France International, National Public Radio and Public Radio International; read about them in The New York Times, International Herald Tribune, The Economist, Financial Times, Africa Today, West Africa; Letters from Mama confirmed all I heard and read. In Gidaland in particular, inflation, hunger, intense feelings of helplessness continued to threaten our people's enduring hope for a better tomorrow. Avarice, corruption, illicit creation of wealth . . . all these were worse than when I was there. General Jéjélayé continued to dominate our people, intimidating, arresting, torturing, jailing, killing dissidents as he had done since he seized power many years ago. The Human Rights Watch World Report of that year reported on the outrageous abuses in Africa. . . .

Miraculously, from the supposedly poor Africa uranium, oil, diamonds, gold, rubber, coffee, cocoa, timber, fisheries and many other crucial natural resources and raw materials continued to be extracted, transported across the sea to satiate the ever growing appetite of Europe, North America, China, Japan, Australia, New Zealand. Poverty, hunger, (inculcation of) fear, scarcity of this and that, guns, ethnic feuds, war, systematic rape and torture and many other manners and instruments of terror continued to plague Africa and her children. Many of them continued to flee to Europe and North America. Besides the natural and mineral resources of Africa, she continued to be desirable to the world only as the cosmic zoo, an extant Garden of Eden. Tourists flocked there to behold the majesty of creation, the natural world on the brink of certain death. The majority of the tourism industry is not owned nor managed by Africans.

In my dejected state I came to believe nothing was going to change in Gidaland, in Africa. . . .

Further depressing me, the most painful injury to my heart: my maternal grandparents died days apart, my grandfather first; my grandmother seven days afterwards. So dear to me they were. Their material and spiritual support had nurtured me from infancy. They were my flowers, who stoically endured the passionate embrace of the (African) sun as they toiled on the farm they started solely to finance my undergraduate education, without which I would not have attended college because Mama—a single mother, her husband, my father, having died while she was still pregnant with me, her only child—simply could not afford it on her meager earning as a seamstress. I agonized, still do, over my not seeing them alive again, never to play with them again, or learn from them again . . . My grandparents gone from this life, taking with them their knowledge of this world, knowledge we the living could use, need in fact. With their departure from this life also passed unrealized my desire to cull their knowledge about our indigenous healing know-how. I had planned someday to sit down with them conversing about and compiling a list of the plants, herbs and roots which heal all kinds of bodily diseases, as they were knowledgeable about them and adept at "folk" medicine. I kept thinking about the last time I saw them alive—when I had gone with Mama to Boyo village, my ancestral homeland where they lived, to see them before I left for America—and wondered what my grandfather meant by a certain prophesy about me coming to pass. Was he referring to my depression in America? Was he referring to an event yet to happen to me? . . . I had looked forward to seeing my grandparents again, spending time with them again, listening anew to my grandfather's ideas on life, learning from his knowledge about the ways of this world . . . I am the first and only college-educated member of my family . . . I am the first and only one who had ventured outside of Gidaland, outside of Africa . . . the first and only one who had the opportunity at a panoramic view of the world, at a panoramic view of the global human family from outside Gidaland, from outside of Africa. I had dreamt of recounting to my grandparents my stay in New York City, a place they cannot locate on the map; they in fact did not know a thing called a map exists. But that was not to be; they were gone. They now reside Elsewhere, never to be seen alive again here in this world. And I was not there to bid them farewell. I was not there to hold their cold hands; caress their serene, lifeless faces; touch their closed eyelids; weep over their still bodies; longingly gaze at them as they were bathed, perfumed, powdered, clothed and laid out in state. I was not there to firmly hold Mama's hand as we gave them back to earth in the adjacent graves dug at the courtyard of their house in Boyo village, near our ancestral shrine, where they had expressed their wish to be laid for their eternal rest. From distant New York City all I did, could do, was send Mama the entire sum needed for their burial. Although the money was half of my monthly stipend from Mrs. Piety, I was all too happy to send it. Apart from being my duty to do so—their one and only grandson; the only other bearer of their genes apart from Mama—it was my only opportunity to pacify the guilt tormenting me for my not being there to bid them farewell. Their deaths caused me the most painful injury, sinking me deeper into my black hole of an existence. . . .

With my world thus shattered, with my having no interest at all in the things and ways of this world, what was I to do? Where else was I to go? Who do I turn to? I was tired of it all, utterly fed up and increasingly thought about doing it.

Having perforated and singed the thick blanket of clouds into pieces gliding across the sky, everyday the sun passionately embraced the city smiling triumphantly, his breath warm. Mesmerized by the passionate embrace of the sun, flowers had opened up wide in unconditional submission of love, willing partners in their eternal cosmic copulation. Trees swayed to the ballad of the wind. The days and nights warmed up. People wore light spring jackets, not bulky long winter coats. They crowded the sidewalks. Delight animated their faces. Their robust laughter rounded their cheeks. Lovers snuggled, their molten eyes locked in alluring gazes. Spring had arrived. I thought of Mika, who was back home in Amsterdam working on her doctoral dissertation proposal. I imagined her holding my hand and gazing into my eyes, our deep kisses steadying our quivering lips.

The liveliness of that spring elevated my spirit somewhat, but the emptiness I felt remained. I continued drinking and smoking, my points of light. Eventually, I decided to do it. The questions were: Where? When? How?

Two incidents occurred that spring. They yanked me out of the black hole, set me free.

The first was this:

Afternoon. Physically, I was in my apartment, in the living room, seated cross legged on the sofa drinking and chain smoking; mentally, I was deep in the black hole, my mind tormented with the questions: where? When? How?

Later that afternoon I left my apartment, and downstairs mumbled a "fine thank you" to Mr. Bill's—one of the doormen of my apartment building, a most pleasant man—- "how you doing?" and walked into the world.

I walked and walked, and eventually came to a bridge underneath which flowed a river. I walked along the bridge fingering the horizontal silver bar barricading passersby from the river. I was alone. It was quiet. I could hear the river murmuring below. I listened more closely and realized the river was whispering to me.

"My child, I know you are hurting. You know no peace. Come make your home with me. I will comfort and protect you. With me, you will have peace. . . .

"My child, I know you are hurting. . . ."

I stood there contemplating the river, my thighs grazing the horizontal bar retaining me in this realm of time called history; separating me from the timeless realm called eternity, the gateway to which was the river below. I stood there contemplating the river . . . climbed and sat on the bar, my feet dangling in space in front of me, the river below a vast sheet of mirror glistening from the rays of the sun. I stared at the mirror. I soon began feeling dizzy and weightless, my image swaying on the mirror. Then, my image changed to others. I saw Gandhi dressed in an immaculate white dhoti, his owlish glasses balanced on the bridge of his nose, his palms pressed together, raised up to his face. I saw Yitzhak Rabin wearing a black suit, his eyes radiant, his hair neatly combed. I saw Martin Luther King, Jr. wearing a blue suit, Harriet Tubman standing at his side. I saw Lumumba wearing a yellow shirt, its front soiled brownish here and there, his hair Afro and kinky. I saw Sankara wearing a green shirt and trousers, smiling blissfully, women wearing bright colored dresses ringed round him, smiling at him. I saw Nkrumah wearing a yellow Mao styled shirt, a green band of kente cloth slung across his chest. I saw Mandela dressed in a green shirt, his hair neatly combed and parted in the middle, his right hand raised, fingers clenched into a tight fist, Winnie Mandela, regally dressed, standing at his right hand side, Miriam Makeba, also regally dressed, standing at his left hand side, all three of them softly singing "Nkosi Sikelel iAfrica" (God Bless Africa). I saw Felá Aníkulápó-Kútì dressed in a yellow body hugging shirt and trousers and shoes, his attire adorned with Yorùbá mythological emblems, his right hand raised, the fingers balled into a taut fist, a fat and long "grass," smoldering, dangling between the fore and middle fingers of his left hand, with Fúnmiláyò Kútì, his mother, standing at his side, her spectacles balanced on the bridge of her nose. . . .

I stared at them in the mirror.

Silence,

But,

The purling river,

And,

Their voices.

I stared at them, listening . . .

Their voices now ended, their images disappeared.

I stared at the river, her call reverberating in my mind: "My child, I know you are hurting. Come make your home with me. I will comfort and protect you."

I moved to answer the call of the river, my feet dangling in space, my arms outstretched, my buttocks slowly but surely slipping off the bar. As I was about to, I heard a cry:

"Nooooo! Òdodo, please don't. Don't quit. I love you. Please don't." Astonished, I grabbed the bar, stared at the mirror, saw Mika dressed in a white robe, her eyes soaked in tears, wriggling down her beautiful face. She again called out to me: "Òdodo, please don't." I grabbed the bar tighter, Mika's voice echoing in my head . . . I got off the bar, walked away from the river, my knees jerking, Mika's words echoing in my head. . . .

Dear to me, Mika. But that had not suppressed my suicidal urge. Having just tried to kill myself, I was overwhelmed with shame for having been unmindful of the voices of my historical ancestors; for having been inconsiderate of the people dear to me, to whom my death would have caused certain pain.

I continued walking, recalling the words of King, Lumumba, Sankara, Nkrumah, Mandela, Felá. They had spoken to me when their images appeared on the mirrored surface of that river.

King:

"Òdodo, the Spirit is in you now. I want you to know that our people will one day be free, and you must play your part in achieving it. That is your destiny. You cannot negate it. You are a soldier for Freedom, for Love. Fear not. The Light is in you. It will eclipse Darkness whenever you encounter It."

Lumumba:

"Òdodo, you must heed what our brother just said. The Spirit is in you now. Freedom will be realized for our people. Love will prevail. And do not forget to laugh. Humor is important even as you slave in your mortal existence."

Sankara:

"Òdodo, listen to me very well. It is your turn to fight for Freedom. The time is now. Not yesterday. Not today. Not tomorrow. Now . . . Freedom will be won for our people. Love will prevail. Do not despair. Have no fear. The Spirit is in you now. And, yes, do not forget to laugh, very important, laughter."

Nkrumah:

"The secret of life is to have no fear. You must remember this always. The life of he who has chosen to seek Knowledge is never an easy one. On his path are innumerable thorns. The life of he who has chosen to be a warrior for Love is a perpetually agony ridden one. You must be strong. There is a purpose for your life. All our hopes are on your generation. You are the ones to improve on our mistakes, learn from our shortcomings, and carry on the struggle to realize freedom for our people. Africa must give birth to Freedom. The wellbeing of all her children all over the world must be accomplished. That requires they must unite, ignore the doubting Thomases among them and sacrifice the Judases. That in turn requires they must be fearless. It never has been and never will be easy, this righteous struggle. The purpose of your life is to partake in it. This purpose you must fulfill. Suicide is not in your destiny. Have no fear. The Spirit is in you now."

Mandela:

"You cannot deny your destiny. You can only delay it. You know the struggle is my life. You know my belief that there is no easy walk to Freedom. You know my belief that realizing freedom for all human beings by fighting the mighty force of Oppression should be the highest aspiration of every man. I submitted to my destiny, and played my part in the struggle. You too should submit and play your part."

Felá's words were vitriolic, but loving. He had stared at me like a bull does a matador, his nose swelling, and said:

"Òdodo, what is wrong with you, eh? You dey craze for head? You no be man? No be African man you be? Why you dey run from life. Why you dey run from the struggle eh? Sebi you claim say you admire me, my courage, the way I lived my life for the struggle. So, wetin you wan kill yourself for? . . . You no be quitter. Na Òdodo be your name. You must carry on O! Die-die no dey for your destiny O! Na compass you be. Na young Afrikan pioneer you be. The Beautyful Ones. Na people like you go show others the way to follow. So, make you stop this suicide nonsense O! Make you dey yansh instead, I beg, fucking is good for the body and the spirit." So, you must fuck well-well O!" he concluded, puffing on his "grass," the fumes eclipsing his face.

Gandhi, smiling, his owlish glasses balanced on the bridge of his nose, his seemingly fragile strong skinny legs sticking out of his dhoti, had simply pressed his palms together, raised it to his face and nodded at me.

Rabin, his eyes radiant like a star, had, also, simply smiled at me.

. . .

As I walked back to my apartment I happened on a café and decided to stay there awhile to contemplate what had just transpired. I ordered a large cup of cappuccino. I fought back the tears threatening to shroud my eyes. My mind was riotous with thoughts. Scenes from my life flashed in my mind's eye. I recalled discovering in the International Herald Tribune Mrs. Piety's announcement of a fully funded graduate school scholarship for "underprivileged students." I recalled having the dispute with Mama when I was applying for the scholarship, in which she tearfully expressed her desire that I study Business Administration not Development Studies as, she believed, the one lucrative and the other not. I recalled reading Mrs. Piety's congratulation letter informing me I had won the scholarship, assuring me of her support given my "superlative" academic achievement at undergraduate study, and a "certain feeling" she had that I was "heading for greatness." I recalled experiencing for the first time in my life a certain pleasure of the flesh with Foláké, my maiden girlfriend. I recalled the farewell ceremony Mama organized for me to wish me well in America and to pray for my safe return. I recalled meeting Mika in Amsterdam while I was en route to New York City. And arriving in New York City, spending my first weeks there walking about discovering the place. . . .

"Your water," the gentle voice of the waitress nudged me out of my recollection. She put a glass on my table. I looked up at her: A charming face, hearty smile.

"Looks like you were meditating," she said, smiling.

"I was just thinking about things in general," smiling, I said.

She nodded. "I understand."

"Thank you for the water."

"You're welcome," she said, the smile still lively on her face.

Her sunny smile warmed me.

It was late afternoon when I left the café. The sun was still smiling on the city.

. . .

The river incident liberated me, revived my urge for life. But, it was to be the first of two incidents that yanked me out of my black hole of an existence.

The second incident occurred the night of that same day. It was this:

I was in my apartment, in the living room, seated cross legged on the sofa, smoking, thinking things over. Drowsy, I extinguished the cigarette and stretched out on the sofa. . . .

A gentle voice now telling me: "Look out the window, look out this moment." I get up, walk to one of the windows overlooking the city. I peer into the night, my breath fogging the windowpane. Amid the dark, starless night, seated low serenely over the city, an alien body watching the earth: the pregnant moon. Enchanted by the calm gaze of the moon, I stand at the window gazing at her . . . I begin to feel a compulsion to walk about the city.

I am roaming the city with no destination in mind . . . now approaching a deserted park, one of its wood and wrought iron benches aglow with the silvery radiance of the moon. I feel compelled to sit on the bench. I reason it is tranquil here, a perfect place to sit awhile, enjoy the gentle breeze. So, I sit on one side of the bench. It is quiet.

I feel compelled to stare at the moon . . . I now feel an eerie atmosphere about me. I turn my gaze from the moon. Seated next to me on the other side of the bench is a woman. I have no idea whence she came. I am sure she was not there earlier. She gazes into my eyes. Captivated, I draw closer to her. The most beautiful woman I have ever laid my eyes upon. She is lean, tall and erect and long limbed. Her lustrous skin is the color of night in a medieval village. Her ethereal looking eyes are luminous, and adorned with thick eyebrows and long eyelashes. Her lips are full, the top lip somewhat upturned, alluring. Her high cheekbones are powdered with gold dust, making them twinkle. She is wearing tiny gold bar earrings dangling on gold chains. On her long gazelle-like neck is a sparkling diamond clustered necklace, its huge diamond pendant nestled in her glorious cleavage, glowing. Covering her lean frame is a flowing, ankle length white linen dress. Wafting from her body the smell of cocoa, coffee, fruits, oil. . . .

I sit on the bench mesmerized, gazing at her. I cannot help ogling her upright breasts: their vigilant nipples are staring at me through the veil of her thin fabric linen dress.

"Such intense gaze," she says. Her voice is nasal, her ivory looking teeth perfect, her tongue pink.

I look away, at my toes.

"Òdodo, feeling depressed of late, eh? Your load is a heavy one, but it is your destiny to carry it."

I am surprised she knows my name.

My Selves are offering their opinions:

"She is a lunatic," my Reason opines.

"Do not listen to that plastic. Hear the woman out," my Intuition counsels.

"You are surprised that I know your name. Do not be afraid, Òdodo, All is well and will be well with you."

She reads minds too?

"I told you she is a lunatic," Reason insists.

"A spirit," Intuition disagrees.

"Her beauty has undermined your rational judgment," Reason refuses to relent.

"You lifeless plastic. You have no soul, that is what your problem is," Intuition rebukes.

With both my Selves battling for my attention, I am confused.

"Òdodo, do not be afraid. I mean you no harm. How

could I harm my own son?"

I am confused about what she means by "How could I harm my own son?" Has Mama died and is, in this woman's form, now appearing to me before she passes on? I remember the stories my maternal grandfather used to tell me about souls who are no longer of the human world yet have not completely departed it, but remain loitering about their loved ones.

"Òdodo, do not worry. Your Mama is well."

"Flee! Now!" Reason tells me.

"Remain. Hear the woman out!" Intuition counsels.

"Òdodo, I have been skulking about this city for some time waiting for you . . ." She looks about the park.

Her choices of words—"skulking about," "waiting for you"—are not lost on me.

"Perhaps she is one of those lonely beautiful women in the city. Perhaps it is your lucky day. No more sleeping alone," Reason whispers to me betraying Its sudden change of opinion, Its fickle disposition.

"WOULD YOU SHUT UP!" Intuition yells.

"Waiting for me?" I murmur.

"Yes, waiting for you," she says gazing at me. "I would have come to you in your apartment, but I wanted us to meet out here in the open," she swings her long arm carving an arch through the air, "and enjoy this enchanted night together." She gazes upward at the moon.

She again looks about the park, her eyes luminous, her hand dangling in mid air, fingers stretched. With her slim fingers she had been etching all kinds of invisible shapes on the dark blanket of night as she talked.

"I am here to help you," she continues. "I know you have been feeling depressed and uninspired lately. I know you have attempted to end your current manifestation in this life by drowning. I know you cannot think things through, struggling to decide what to do now that you have dropped out of school."

I sit listening to her, awed by her presence.

"Òdodo, the purpose of this world" she continues "is to realize Universal Freedom, to realize Love. And only a few are gifted with an intuitive knowledge of this and will play a major role in the daunting struggle to realize it. You are one of them. This is why you are introspective and empathic. It is why you detest all manners of domination. It is why you are thoughtful and provoke thought. In my house, the struggle for Freedom, for Love, continues. You yourself know that since they first beheld me, my sunny existence and warmth and beauty have enraptured them. They have repeatedly raped me. And the abuse persists. Some of my children have joined them in molesting me. And the loyal ones who revolted against this injustice and became devoted fighters for my liberation have perished in the struggle, many of them murdered, Lambs sacrificed on the altar of History that I am. But they did not die in vain because you, and others like you, my loyal children, The Beautyful Ones Who Are Now Born, have been infused with the Spirit and will carry on the struggle until I am truly liberated.

"Òdodo, you have the intuition of your purpose, your destiny. It is to partake in the struggle for my emancipation. The struggle to realize genuine and lasting freedom for all my children including those who were stolen from me and scattered all over the world, and those yet unborn. And beyond that, your destiny is to partake in the struggle to realize Freedom, to realize Love in the world of mortals, for all mortals. It is a daunting task because Evil is powerful, Its mortal agents are thoroughly armed. But they will be defeated.

"And I know that you have not fully submitted to It, but you must understand that your soul has now chosen the Pen as your tool in the struggle. The Pen is a powerful tool, a mighty Sword with which to slay Domination, with which to carve the path to Truth. You must grab the Pen and begin to wield It ceaselessly."

She gazes into my eyes. I feel an intense energy transmitting from her into me. She strokes my cheek. Her touch is feathery, cold.

"Òdodo, you cannot deny your destiny, you hear?"

I nod.

"You are one of my loyal sons. I am sure the meaning of this encounter has infused your mind. Now, you know that your reason for being is to partake in the battle for my freedom. You are a messenger. The Pen is your Sword. Be strong. Your future is full of struggle. You must conquer fear. Like tonight, you need not have been scared of me. Nothing will happen to you that is not fated. That is why you must endeavor to listen less to that voice of Reason in your head. Although they are yet to realize it, Reason is both the light and darkness of mortals. Òdodo, if you must listen to Reason do so with your Heart. Listen more to your Intuition from now onward. It will never deceive you. You hear?"

I nod.

"And, most importantly, walk with your eyes open. You will begin to recognize their symbols and decipher its hidden meaning."

I nod.

"Your path is already cleared for you. As you continue on your journey in this life, you will meet many mortals who will help you. They will reveal themselves to you. They will provide you with all that you will need to fulfill your destiny."

I nod.

"There is so much more to tell you, but what I have said will do for the moment."

She looks about the park.

"I will appear to you whenever you need me and when I need you."

I nod.

"Be strong. Be brave. The battle you must partake in is a daunting one. But you will triumph. Although your body will be conquered, your spirit will triumph."

I nod.

Silence.

I am thinking about what she said just now: Although my body will be conquered, my spirit will triumph.

"So long, my child," she now says gazing into my eyes. I feel a glow radiate in me.

She gets up. I stare at Her as she glides into the night, noticing her feet are not touching the ground.

I continue to stare at Her as she glides into the night

and, simply, disappears.

My Selves continue warring:

"It is ridiculous to think anything of it. You are simply dreaming," Reason sternly reprimands me.

"Do not listen to that fraud, that soulless plastic. You should listen to the woman," Intuition implores me.

I sit on the bench grateful she had come to completely yank me out of the black hole, to remind me of my life's work, to counsel me on my ongoing reflection on changing my academic discipline.

I get up from the bench leaving the park, Her voice in my head: "You are a messenger. You must conquer fear. Nothing will happen to you that is not fated. That is why you must endeavor to listen less to that voice of Reason in your head. Although they are yet to realize it, Reason is both the light and darkness of mortals. Òdodo, if you must listen to Reason, do so with your Heart. From now onward listen more to your Intuition, heed Its voice, It will never deceive you."

I woke up feeling a renewed zeal for life.

Mika had called overnight and left a message: she had "a strange dream, very troubling. You were thrashing about desperately in a river, and I dived in and saved you." I recalled her apparition on that river's mirrored surface begging me not to jump: "Nooooo! Òdodo please don't. Don't quit. I love you. Please don't." An intense energy had jolted me upon seeing her form, fortifying my intuition that there was a Force, a magnetic Pull, attracting us to each other. She had been in my thoughts since I arrived in New York City. I was sure I loved her. But I had not been forthright about it in my conversations and correspondences—which, pathetic of me (or was it caution, shyness?), were mostly of the intellectual sort—-with her since I arrived in New York City. Besides talking on the telephone, we had communicated via mail. Longhand letters we both enjoy writing and cherish receiving; greeting cards we both love sending and collecting.

I called her back. Although we had a long conversation, I did not tell her anything about my suicide attempt. I simply was too ashamed to do so. Later that morning I decided to go to the neighborhood café for brunch.

I ordered a cup of coffee and cheesecake, wriggled into a comfortable position on the metallic, bistro styled chair, my notepad—my constant companion into which I immortalize my ideas and which I had neglected since my descent into the black hole—-folded back onto a blank page, my pen poised.

The apparition of Africa in the form of that regal woman fortified my urge for living, propelled me on the arduous journey of self-assessment I must endure so as to arrive at a decision on the new focus of my formal education and career thereafter.

I sat thinking about my itching desire to change my discipline. I had no doubt I must change the focus of my graduate school education from Development Studies, away from academic social sciences altogether. I no longer wanted to seek Knowledge through it given that I had, finally, come to comprehend it to be about social engineering of human societies, not about truly seeking knowledge on how a society achieves development, which, profoundly understood, is the issue of how a society comes into being and sustains itself. Knowledge on how to achieve the development of a society is what I had long yearned for, it is what I had long believed would help me understand how Gidaland, how Africa can achieve genuine and lasting development and prosperity, thus bettering the lives of our people. I must seek that knowledge elsewhere. Where, I was not sure. And what should be the new focus of my formal education? What should be the career I wholeheartedly dedicate my life to? I was sure of one thing: the career I choose must be in public service.

I sat hunched over the table of the café, cross legged, my knees grazing its round edge, scrawling in my notepad, my pen a dagger lacerating the heart of my existential predicament. New Yorkers strolling by; delight seated on their faces. My coffee yawning in my face, my cheesecake now a truncated triangle, beside which rests my cheesecake smeared fork. I continued to scrawl my mind, recalling Africa's words: "And I know that you have not fully submitted to It, but you must understand that your soul has now chosen the Pen as your tool in the struggle. The Pen is a powerful tool, a mighty Sword with which to slay Domination, with which to carve the path to Truth. You must grab the Pen and begin to wield It ceaselessly."

The whole of academia uses the pen. Which discipline in particular was Africa referring to? What ought to be my new graduate school discipline?

I left the café energized and infused with Hope.

## Rendezvous with My Destiny

It was a Thursday night. I was here in the bungalow draped loincloth style in one of the white linen wrappers Mama had sewn for me to use as cover-clothes (blankets), which still smelled sweetly of Mika from our love dance of the previous night and of early that morning. Miles Davis was in the background passionately toning his Sketches of Spain. A cup of Kenyan coffee warming my palms, steaming my face, I stood observing the world through a window in my living room. A light breeze cooled the night. Trees whistled softly. Silhouettes of people danced on flapping window curtains of some of the houses on my street. The pregnant moon sat serenely gazing at the world.

I stood observing the night, softly whistling along with Miles, intermittently sipping coffee and thinking about the article I was working on before I came to indulge in a reverie by the window. I had taken leave of the article to mull an idea.

As I stood there watching the night an idea suddenly banged at the door of my consciousness. Ah, the divine nature of Thought, I said, and walked back to my study. I sat at my desk, hunched over the article, my pen rapidly scraping my notepad, devouring its blank space.

Not long after I had begun writing knocks on my front door interrupted my thought-flow. Mika had left here that afternoon and was back in Freedom House, our home in Boyo Village, for the weekend. I was to join her and Mama there the next afternoon. I expected no one, so the knocking was an annoying distraction. I remained hunched over my desk thinking who it could be, my right hand motionless in space, my pen looking back at me expectantly, the Lambs—a collage of Socrates, Jesus, Gandhi and Martin Luther King, Jr.—-hanging on the wall in front of me gazing at me, my desktop lamp glowing, the only lighting alive in my study . . . More knocks on the door. I got up and walked to the window where I had earlier stood and spied on the night. Standing outside was a man unfamiliar to me. He was tall and muscular. There was a bulge in the left breast pocket of his tailored suit. On the street behind him waited a sleek black Mercedes-Benz. Two brawny men in suits sat inside the car: one at the steering wheel, the other on the front passenger seat. Their demeanor hinted at their identity. I tiptoed back to my study, switched on my micro-tape recorder, hid it behind some literature on the shelf and turned on the overhead light in my study and in the living room.

I slightly opened the door grabbing its knob and peered outside.

"May I help you?"

The man dug his hand into his breast pocket, and held a government security card in front of my face. "The General sent me to get you, sir," he said.

"The General sent for me?"

"Yes, sir."

My first thought was to call Mika to let her know.

"I need to make a call."

"Sorry sir, but I am under order not to let you use the telephone, sir."

"Is that so?"

"Yes, sir."

Perhaps it was my turn; perhaps another son of Africa was about to be slain; another Lamb sacrificed on the Altar of History that Africa is, I thought.

"I need to dress," I said, pointing to my wrapper.

"I have to wait with you inside, sir."

"Okay," I said, relaxing my grip on the knob, opening the door wider.

He entered.

"Have a seat."

"I am okay, sir."

He stood in the middle of the living room, his head almost touching the ceiling. I went into the bedroom, and left the door slightly opened so I could spy on him as I dressed. He paced about the living room, intermittently slyly observing me as I changed into khaki trousers, wrinkled cotton shirt and Bierkenstock sandals.

"I have to search you, sir . . . just a security measure, sir," he said when I joined him in the living room. He ran his palms over me—from my shoulders to my wrists, my chest down to my ankles. He found only my bunch of keys and wallet, poked his fingers about in its compartment and handed it to me.

I wondered what to make of the whole affair as we walked toward my front door. The respect with which the man treated me was baffling. Besides his addressing me with the venerable "sir," he treated me kindly; his companions had remained in the car the whole time; the bungalow was not sacked; the article I was writing was not scrutinized and confiscated; I was allowed to gather the manuscript and my writing materials and put them in my desk drawer. Given that cordial handling, this is nothing to be alarmed about, I assured myself as I locked my door. Besides, "You must conquer fear. Nothing will happen to you that is not fated," is what Africa had told me in New York City, I reminded myself as we walked to the Mercedes-Benz.

The man opened and held the car door, and ushered me inside with a wave of his hand. "Mind your head, sir," he cautioned me as I got into the car. He followed, bending low, and sat to the right of me. "Another security measure, sir," he said and blindfolded me. "Move!" he said to the driver, his voice stern. The sleek car purred, eased into gear and glided into the night, hugging the smooth asphalt. "My apology for the blindfold, sir. I have my orders," he said. "I understand," I said. Silence. Then, I heard a ruffling sound, as if he were searching in his pocket, and the press of a button. "We are on our way, sir," he said. He did not say anything more. I felt him shift in his seat as he made himself comfortable beside me. Silence; except the droning of the air conditioner of the car.

With me securely in its arms, the car hurried into the night. Where to?

I tried to mentally map the direction we were traveling. My effort was frustrated as the car made numerous abrupt stops and turns. I thought of Mika and Mama. What would become of them if my abduction was indeed a master plan of the General's and I was never seen alive again? I sat still, the car hurrying into the night. Just then, the image of Abdul flashed in my mind's eye, his hand raised, fingers balled into a fist in the unmistakable black power salute like Mandela, like Felá . . . Then, the image of Africa, regal in her flowing, thin shoulder strap white linen dress, smiling, gazing into my eyes, saying "I am here for you, my child. No need to fear." What more reassurance could I wish for? I straightened my upper body, and sat erect against the car's plush seat.

After about an hour of driving, the car slowed, and stopped. I heard a buzz, followed by what sounded like a gate opening. The car slowly continued. I realized the car was riding on a graveled path given the grinding noise the tire made, and deduced we had entered through a gate into the compound of a house. The car stopped. "Mind your head, sir," the man said to me as he held my wrist and led me out of the car, the blindfold still tight on my eyes. A gentle breeze caressed my face. We were walking on the graveled path, trees were chattering. His pace slowed. "Just a moment, sir," he said. I heard a buzz, and the sound of a door opening. "Mind your head, sir," he again said as we walked through the door, my wrist in his hand. We kept walking, our footsteps reverberating, the sounds hollow. His steps slowed, his grip on my wrist loosened. He stopped. "Sir, I am going to remove the blindfold," he said.

I found myself inside a brightly lit winding corridor with cameras built into the wall at short intervals. Walking side by side we navigated the corridor and eventually came to a dead end, and had to make a right turn. We came to a floor-to-ceiling glass-door. "After you, sir," bowing, he ushered me in with a wave of his hand.

The door automatically slid apart as I approached it. I walked into a spacious windowless air-conditioned room, its thickly padded walls painted white. An incredibly long L shaped beige leather sofa in a section of the room backing a wall. On the wall the sofa backed three big black masks staring at the onlooker. A map of the world atop which sat an eagle dominated the length of the wall on the right side of the sofa. In front of the stately sofa an enormous marble-based reflective dark-glass top rectangular coffee table. On it a gold-colored tin box, a marble ashtray and a black remote control device. Imposing on the floor directly across from the sofa a sleek flat-screen black monitor with a red light at its base, blinking. At a corner of the room a semicircular marble bar, on its countertop bottles of assorted foreign drinks, nearby a tall stainless steel refrigerator, lustrous.

Seated on the sofa, cigar smoke undulating in front of his intent eyes, hugging his face, was General Jéjélayé, the, so called, leader of Gidaland, who had dominated our people for such a long time now. The man famous for being a recluse, whose image I, like most of our people, knew only through his communiqués on television, and the photographs of him published in local and foreign newspapers. His elusiveness and secrecy earned him a nickname: the Sphinx. He rarely appeared in public and rarely spoke to journalists except during his erratic news conferences, which I had started attending in my capacity as an international affairs journalist covering his office for the Ecumenical Society in New York soon after I arrived back here in Gidaland. He had haunted my dreams and thought since I was a youngster. He continued to haunt my dreams and my thoughts when I was in New York doing graduate work in Development Studies, especially during my black hole days there. He continued to haunt me even when I had stopped worrying over the issue of Development, having changed my focus from Development Studies to International Affairs Journalism. I had repeatedly called him a leech, the cunning perpetrator of the miserable existence afflicting the majority of our people. There I was in front of him, meeting him in person alone for the first time.

The General looked regal in a black *agbádá* made of silk with intricate gold embroidery at the neck, wrists and ankles.

The man who had brought me to the General stood rigid at my side. The General looked at him and nodded. He turned to face me, searched me as he had in the bungalow. He again found only my keys and wallet, poked his fingers about in its compartments. He looked at the General. The General nodded. He handed me my keys and wallet. "That would be all, Ibrahim," the General said to him, and pressed some numbers on the remote. I got the numbers except one. The door slid apart. Ibrahim exited the room. The General again pressed some numbers on the remote control, the two halves of the door slid shut. I got all the numbers this time and memorized them. The same combination opens and closes the door. Not terribly smart, I thought.

"Good evening, your Excellency," I said, bowing.

He surprised me when, smiling, he stood and held out his right hand. I shook it. It was surprisingly soft like that of a toddler.

"Welcome to my refuge. Please, sit down." He pointed to the sofa as he sat back in its middle. I sat on the tail of the sofa's L shape, so that we sat facing each other at an angle. Facing us was the sleek monitor, the red light at its base still blinking.

"My apology for the blindfold, the searches . . . the precautions one must make. I am sure you understand."

I was surprised he apologized to me.

"Of course I understand, your Excellency. One cannot be too careful, especially a man as yourself."

He gazed at me.

"Do you always speak your mind fearlessly?"

I nodded. "And I know when to be tactful."

He continued to gaze at me.

"You are a very intelligent man, and observant. I know you have already memorized the combination to my door. But I change it daily." He smiled, and picked up the tin box from atop the coffee table, the diamond-ring on his finger sparkling. "Cigar?"

"I thank you for offering, but I do not smoke."

"Never?"

"I smoked cigarettes briefly in New York."

"How about some cognac and nuts? Nuts are good for you and the cognac will relax you. In fact I can use a drink myself."

"I prefer red wine, but I will have some cognac with you."

"So, drink wine. There is plenty."

"So kind of you, but the cognac is okay."

"As you wish," he said, smiling.

Why is he being jovial with me? What is he up to? I thought.

The General pressed some numbers on the remote and turned his gaze at the monitor, the red light at its base now no longer blinking. A man walking toward the door appeared on the monitor. He was dressed in a white shirt and trousers and wore white gloves. He held his right arm bent at the elbow, a white napkin balanced on it. He now waited in front of the door. The General pressed the combination, the door slid open. The man entered, the door slid shut behind him. The General again pressed numbers on the remote, the monitor went blank and its red light resumed blinking. The man stood facing the General his head bent downward. "Bring us some cognac and nuts," the General said to him. The servant walked to the bar, the napkin still balanced on his arm. He brought back to us a golden tray. On it were three goblets, an unopened bottle of cognac, a crystal bowl and a nylon packet on which was written "Mixed Nuts." He put the tray down gingerly on the coffee table, his gentle face looking back at him from atop the table's glass. The General was intently watching him as he rubbed the goblets with the napkin, opened the cognac and poured some into one of the goblets. He emptied the packet of "Mixed Nuts"—a combination of groundnut, cashew and almond—into the crystal bowl, scooped a handful of the nuts and dumped it into his mouth. He chewed gracefully. The General continued watching him. He swallowed the nuts, picked up the goblet with the cognac in it, raised it to his lips and drank elegantly. He gently returned the goblet onto the tray, and stood facing the General. The General stared at him. I watched them both. The General's fixed look at his servant, the latter's graceful expression as he stood waiting. The room was completely silent. The silence was deafening, intimidating; all sorts of possibilities lurked in it. After staring at his servant awhile, the General shifted in his seat, a gentle smile softening his face. He nodded to the servant. With a goblet balanced on the palm of his gloved hand, the servant poured and bowing handed the General a drink. He poured another drink and bowing handed it to me. Then, his head somewhat bent he stood facing the General. The General nodded. The servant again bowed and headed for the door. The General pressed the combination, the door opened. The servant disappeared into the corridor. The General again pressed the combination closing the door.

"To one of our foremost thinkers," the General said, his goblet raised.

"To critical thinking," I said, raising my goblet.

The cognac—biting the walls of my mouth, my tongue—tasted good. I let it linger in my mouth awhile before swallowing.

"I am glad you could come," he said.

"Not that I had any choice," I said.

"I see you are a man of humor."

"With the miserable condition of the majority of our people, that is very important to a man these days."

"I will drink to that." As he touched the goblet to his lips, he stared into my eyes. I felt him responding to me psychically, telling me my remark was not lost on him.

"Your Excellency, with all due respect, may I ask why you had me brought here?"

"Oh, for no reason in particular. Just to chat with you . . . I like you. I appreciate your insistence on asking challenging questions at my news conferences even though you know I will mostly ignore them. It shows your genuine interest in getting at the heart of issues, your genuine interest in the progress of our people . . . You do not flinch in my presence like the others do. It shows you are not afraid of me. I like that. It draws me to you . . . Maybe you can teach me the secret of how you get to be so brave." He smiled.

"Secret?"

He nodded.

"There is no secret. I just do not dwell on my physical safety . . . My friend, Ségun, a writer in New York, my other self, in fact, says that one is going to die anyway, so why fear? He is right, of course. So, I just do what I must do."

Silent, he puffed on his cigar and stared into space, smoke thinly veiling his face.

"Your Excellency, I am flattered . . ."

"What do you mean?" He interrupted me.

"I suppose not too many people get to sit with your Excellency in this your cozy sanctuary, definitely not a journalist."

"That is true. But, Òdodo, you are not just any person. You are special, very special." He squinted as he said that, his bushy, graying eyebrows grazing his eyelashes. "The wonderful work you are doing for our people through your Center . . . selling foodstuff cheaply in needy neighborhoods, offering after-school tutorials to youngsters, feeding them . . . that is very admirable of you, godly work you are doing . . . And your ideas, your personality, your aura draw me to you . . . as if you were a Spirit in human form."

"Maybe I am."

He gazed at me.

"Your Excellency, you said the work I am doing with the Center is wonderful." He nodded. "So, why have you not done likewise?"

Silent, he puffed on his cigar and stared into space.

I thought about his comment on my ideas. Nothing about his public life suggested he was intellectually inclined. So, I was surprised he alluded to my ideas. More so because of this: my work outside of journalism is not published here in Gidaland, but in the United States and in Europe. The only work I publish here are articles in the weekly *Voice of Hope*, in which I muse on the state of the country, share my ideas on "pathways" to the progress of the country, a better life for our people, the majority, who continued to be plagued by utter poverty.

"Yes, Òdodo, you definitely are special," he now said.

"I thank you for your kind comment, your Excellency. And, you mentioned my ideas, what about them?"

"Your essays clearly show your intellect, your heart, your love for our people, your love for Africa . . . And although your articles in that column your write in the *Voice of Hope* engage issues on a universal level, they are often critical of my government. I should be enraged, but the truth is I am not. In fact, the whole of your work fascinates me . . . I am not going to completely bare my soul to you in one night of conversation, but I will tell you this: I particularly like your essay, *The Two Kinds of Persons*. There is another one . . ." He squinted as he tried to remember. "Ah, yes, *The March of History amid Us*." He raised his goblet to his lips, gulped the cognac remaining in it.

I was surprised he knew of those essays. How did he come upon them? Why did he seek them? What about them interest him? Was he a closet intellectual?

"What is most interesting to me about those essays is that for once an intellectual is truly aiming to surpass the inclination most of you have for blaming, for naming names, for pointing fingers . . . propaganda disguised as serious thought. But you, you rise above all that. You write on the human condition from a universal perspective. That is the kind of work I would labor to write if I were a man of letters."

It dawned on me just then that of course the General could secure my writings any time he wanted.

What to make of the General's familiarity with my work. If he had recently garnered my work to inspect, it must be intentional, perhaps to investigate me to determine if I am a potential threat. Africa's voice echoed in my head: "You must conquer fear. Nothing will happen to you that is not fated."

"Let us discuss *The Two Kinds of Persons*. I like your implicit idea in it on the need for personal transformation. Although it is not easy to achieve in this day and age . . ."

"I really do not like to discuss my work. The essay speaks for itself. I prefer to let my work continue to do that."

"You are being cautious, eh? I assure you, we are merely having an informal conversation."

"Can you blame me? We live under a certain atmosphere, a cloud of fear," I said, staring at him.

"That troubles you, eh? Your questions during my press sessions, and your articles clearly show that you are not pleased with the situation of things here."

"The majority of our people are fearful to speak of their frustration. They continue to languish in poverty, while you and your comrades are living the good life." I looked round his posh villa-den, the well-stocked bar. “Of course, it saddens me . . . It should sadden anyone who truly loves our people, who truly wants our progress. I love our people. I want us to do well . . . I want our people to have a say in what affects their lives, their wellbeing . . .”

The General shifted his weight on the sofa, and crossed his legs, a grin on his face.

“That kind of comment is what I like so much about you. Deep, truthful, straightforward . . . I want you to share your opinion with me on what you think is wrong with our country?” He took the tin box from atop the coffee table, took a cigar from it, bit off its tip and lit it, puffing on it repeatedly.

Silent, I smiled, looking him straight in the eye, thinking: you damn well know what is wrong with the country, so stop playing with me.

“This cognac is really good,” I said, lifting the goblet to my lips.

“You are ignoring my question . . . you are being careful,” he said, gazing at me.

Silent, I maintained his gaze.

“Well, I am glad you came. We will do this again some time,” he finally said.

We both stood. He held out his hand; I shook it, firmly.

“Thank you for the drink. Good cognac. And the nuts too.”

He ignored my comment.

“I want this meeting to remain a private matter. Not a word to anyone,” he said, staring into my eyes, tightening his grip of my hand. I imagined him telling me: You know the consequence of going against what I just said. But I did not let him win the psychological battle. As he had tightened his grip of my hand, I also had tightened my grip of his hand, maintaining his gaze, intent on gaining the psychological edge, reminding him that, yes, I am not fearful of him at all. “I like you. But certain things must not be transgressed. I want this meeting to remain a private affair. Not a word to anyone,” he said, confirming my deduction of what he was thinking.

“I am a private man, your Excellency. If it becomes

public knowledge, I would not be the guilty man," I said, maintaining his intent gaze.

"Good. I will send for you again. Maybe soon."

"If I am in the country, I will be glad to join you, your Excellency."

"Fair enough." He released my hand and sat back on the sofa.

The General pressed some numbers on the remote control. Ibrahim, who had picked me up at my bungalow, appeared on the monitor and was soon standing in front of the door. The General pressed the combination. The door slid open. Ibrahim entered. The door slid shut behind him. "Your Excellency," he said bowing. The General nodded at him.

I left the room with Ibrahim leading the way. The General remained seated on the sofa clutching the remote, puffing on his cigar. The door slid open as we neared it. We walked into the winding corridor. Ibrahim faced me. "Sir, I am going to . . ." I held up my hand palm up, interrupting him. "Do your duty," I said. He blindfolded me, held my wrist and led me through the corridor. I knew we had gotten to the car when he said, "Mind your head, sir."

The car hurried into the night.

. . .

"I will remove the blindfold now, sir," Ibrahim said. I deduced we must be nearing my neighborhood.

Ibrahim got out of the car, walked round its back to my right side passenger door, opened and held the door for me. "Mind your head, sir," he said as I exited the car.

Windows of the houses on my street were already shut, their curtains drawn. A lone radio from one of the houses was talking to the night.

The ride back took about half hour, half the time it had taken to drive to the General's villa-den. Ibrahim and his men must have driven a circuitous route when they drove me to the General so as to confuse me. That would explain the abrupt stops and turns the driver made, which had undermined my attempt to mentally map the direction we were traveling.

"Thank you for the kind treatment," I said to Ibrahim

in front of my door, looking him in the eyes.

"That was my order, sir. Good night, sir," he said and bowed.

I stood watching him walk back to the car, thinking about his response. 'That was my order, sir', he had said. Meaning if his order had been to brutalize me, that is exactly what he would have done. Military mentality: follow orders, ask no questions. Meaning one must suspend one's moral judgment.

Mika had called, each time leaving a message. Her last message betrayed her panic at my "unusual" disappearance: "Angel, where are you? It's my fifth call. You didn't mention that you'll be going out . . . I'm sure you're fine though . . . Please call me as soon as you get in . . . Bye love."

I retrieved the voice recorder I had hidden behind some literature on the shelf. It had eavesdropped on my conversation with Ibrahim when he had come to take me to the General. If anything had happened to me Mika would have known to check it.

"Hello," Mika said answering her cellular phone on its first ring.

"How are . . ."

"Angel! Where were you?" She interrupted me.

"I went out. Work related."

"Is everything okay?"

"I am an African journalist in Africa. I am sure you understand."

"Yes, dear, I understand."

"All is well. Nothing to worry about," I said not wanting to talk about my meeting with the General. Who knows, perhaps my phone conversations are just then vulnerable.

"I'll see you tomorrow?"

"Yes, tomorrow afternoon."

"Try not to come too late."

"You have a surprise for me?"

"Maybe."

"I love you."

"I love you too."

"Bye, dear."

"Bye, love."

. . .

Unable to readily fall asleep I sprawled on the bed gazing at the ceiling, my mind heavy with thoughts on the meaning of my meeting with the General. What is to come of it? Is he genuinely seeking friendship with me? And why? If he is genuinely seeking my friendship, it may be a divine opportunity for me to affect his thoughts and deeds . . . Could I really effect a transformation in a cunning dictator? . . . I held the bed sheet to my nose. Mika's sweet smell, succor for my tensed nerves. I imagined her coiled up next to me, her head resting on my heart.

I woke early the next morning, finished the article I was writing when Ibrahim and his men had picked me up and later that afternoon drove home to Freedom House, eager to see Mika, and Mama.

Mika met me at the front gate. We kissed and held each other tightly. I felt her heart throbbing. She looked inquiringly into my eyes. I smiled. "All is well," I said, and kissed her. She reached over my shoulder and took my knapsack. Our hands entwined, she led me along the graveled footpath in the middle of our front garden, leading to our front door. Alive, the garden: flowers, flowers and more flowers, colorful, wide eyed, smiling blissfully at the world. Mika kissed me when we got to the front door, held my wrist and led me inside the house, through the hallway, straight to our bedroom.

We have a small collapsible wooden bistro styled table and chairs we use for picnics. Mika had set them in our bedroom. She had adorned the top of the charming table with a white linen tablecloth. In the middle of the table sat a bouquet of flowers, looking lovely in a bronze vase, and a bottle of wine, the wine opener beside it. On the table in front of each of the chairs were an empty glass-jar, an empty plate, a pair of chopsticks, a glass of water and a folded white linen napkin. Nina Simone was in the background singing "Here Comes the Sun."

I stood admiring everything, smiling.

"This is lovely. Thank you," I said, and kissed her.

She pulled one of the chairs from under the table. "Sit here," she said patting the cushioned seat. I sat. "Open the wine. I'll be right back," she said and rushed out of the room. I brought my nose close to the flowers, savored their sweet smell. Metallic noises now reverberated from the kitchen. I opened the wine and gently sat it back on the table to breathe awhile.

Seated at the table waiting for her to return, I thanked Heaven for sending me to New York City via Amsterdam where I met this woman called Mika and now have her in my life.

Mika now re-entered the room carrying one of our glazed ceramic serving pots, gifts from her mother, spaghetti steaming in it. She had cooked the spaghetti directly in home-made spicy tomato sauce, with chunks of fresh tomato, fresh shrimp and cutlets of smoked salmon. This is my favorite of the dishes she makes. She calls it "Spaghetti Africaine." And likes to say it is her "Africanization of spaghetti." As she dished the food, the spaghetti squirmed, fighting against her deft swirling motion to move some of it from the pot to the plates. She served it with a side dish of assorted steamed vegetables.

"Where is Mama?"

"She's visiting Auntie Jùmòké." Auntie Jùmòké is a widow and Mama's friend here in the village. "She said she would be back late if she decides to braid her hair. She told me to come get her when you arrive. She was worried when I couldn't get you on the phone yesterday."

"No need to disturb them. I will spend time with her when she gets back."

She nodded.

I poured some wine into our glass-jars.

"To us," I said raising my jar.

"I celebrate your courage. To your safety, always," she said raising her jar.

"Thank you, dear."

We kissed, sipped our wine.

"Let's eat. I'm starving," she said. Her expression became serious as she concentrated on the steaming plate of spaghetti in front of her, as if it was all that mattered just then.

"Dear, you did not give me a fork."

"Try the chopsticks."

"The stuff is hard to use."

"Angel, just try. Hold it like this."

I tried to hold the chopsticks like she just showed me. One of them fell to the floor.

"It's hopeless. I've been teaching you to use chopsticks since New York. You just refuse to try."

"My ancestors used their fingers, not chopsticks." I stuck out my tongue at her.

Smiling, she gently slapped me on my head, and left the room.

She returned with and handed me a fork.

"This is very good. This meal is a winner always," I said between mouthfuls.

"Made just for you, my dear," she said, slick spaghetti with chunks of tomato clinging to it wound round her chopsticks.

I smiled at her, grateful for her comment.

"The shrimp is so juicy," I said.

"Mama bought it at the river this morning," she said.

"You ought to run a café in the city. This your spaghetti Africaine is really delicious. I owe you a good meal too," I said reaching for my jar of wine.

"You owe me more than a good meal," she said, smiling.

"Oh, you read my mind. I was just about to add a more interesting suggestion."

"And what might that be?"

I smiled, filled our jars with the rest of the wine.

We continued eating.

"That is it for me. I'm full . . . not sure I can get up now," Mika said, rubbing her belly.

"Me too. I have an idea."

"What?"

"I clear the table, leave the dishwashing for later, open another bottle of wine and we lie down for a while."

"That's a great idea."

In bed, Mika's warm, silken body titillating me, her hands round my neck, mine round her waist . . . Kissing . . . White cotton V neck tee shirt, blue ankle length linen skirt, white cotton-brassiere and underwear . . . White cotton long-sleeved shirt, khaki trousers, white cotton boxer shorts, all yanked off heated bodies, dumped in a heap on the floor. Lips quivering. Deep kisses. Dracula bite on her neck . . . Eager tongue, mine, slithering down her stomach,

circuitously caressing her deep seated navel, tracing her velvety pelvic triangle, slithering toward the entrance of her glistening aromatic house of pleasure hidden behind soft, knotty hair . . . Sweet salty taste . . . She murmuring: "Yes, Angel" . . . Tongue slithering upward, nibbling her navel; slithering upward, encountering her nipples . . . She moaning, crawling her fingertips on my chest, my lower back, gently pushing me down on her . . . She gasping, moaning, grunting, babbling, her face contorted with pleasure . . . She now jerking underneath me . . . Me murmuring: "My flower, my flower"; "Yes, Angel. Come Angel," she saying, kissing my face, my neck, her soft palms caressing my behind . . . Me again murmuring: "My flower . . . my flower . . ." Me grunting . . . now jerking atop her.

. . .

"Angel, make love to me like that again. I want to experience that feeling again," Mika now said, eyes shining.

I smiled at her, kissed her, tongued her neck.

"Oh God, no. Not now. I'm still giddy from that one," she said, smiling, snuggled me tighter.

. . .

"Angel, I want to talk about last night," Mika now said.

I had forgotten about the General. Whenever I am with Mika, wrapped in her warm embrace, her soft palm caressing my neck, arousing in me emotion beyond description, my worries dissipate.

We both sat up in bed. I sat with my legs apart, my back against the wall, my head grazing our windowsill overlooking out garden, Mika's pet garden really, at the back of the house. Mika sat between my legs, her legs crossed under her, her cheek resting on my chest, her breath warming my heart.

"Sorry I did not tell you where I was when I called," I said stroking her neck.

"It was clear that you didn't want to discuss it. I knew you were being cautious."

"You would not believe what happened."

"I've thought about some possibilities . . . unexpected meeting with your colleagues . . . the General called another impromptu news conference . . . that's it, isn't it?" She raised her cheek off my chest, gazed at me.

"No."

She replaced her cheek on my chest.

I told her about how Ibrahim and his men showed up at the bungalow, and recounted my conversation with the General, mentioning that before I parted company with him, he warned me not to tell anyone about the meeting.

Silent, she sat curled-up between my legs, caressing my chest.

"So you don't know the location of the place," she now said.

"No. But I suspect it is not far from the bungalow given the time it took them to drive me back."

"It's a hideout."

"Oh, definitely. That explains the blindfold."

"What do you think he's up to?"

"I am not sure. He did say he would like to see me again, so I think it will become clear eventually."

"Could it be that he's trying to see where you are? . . . trying to determine whether you are a threat . . . or maybe . . . no, that can't be it . . ."

"Be what? What were you going to say?"

"It's far-fetched, but I was thinking it could be that his intention is good . . . that he truthfully wants to know your thoughts on the situation here . . . although that's really stretching it."

"I do not think you are stretching it at all. In fact, my intuition tells me he is undergoing a transformation . . . the guy might be experiencing a change of heart. So, you could be right about his intention being genuine. And I do not mean to be romantic about this, but his name is Jéjélayé. As you know, according to our worldview a name signifies the bearer's predetermined earthly demeanor. So, for example, my lot in life is to be truth loving, knowledge seeking, and inspire them in others. To do otherwise would mean that I have abandoned my destiny . . . In the case of the General, his name, Jéjélayé, means benign living, signifying that the bearer will be humble and will have an easy-going disposition . . . That is quite contrary to the demeanor of a dictator . . . I do not know what happened to the General, but it is clear that he has been alienated from his destiny."

"He obviously has strayed from his destiny given his iron-fisted rule all these years. But one should never give up on people like him. Perhaps you're right about his experiencing a transformation. That's why I think his intention for wanting to see you privately is probably sincere."

I nodded.

We both sat lost in thought, Mika's head resting on my heart, me massaging her scalp, caressing her neck.

We now heard Mama's light footsteps in the hallway. (The two women closest to me are graceful walkers. They glide over the ground rather than assault it with the soles of their feet. Sharing a house with them, a writer could not be more fortunate.)

"Tòkunbò! Òdodo!" Mama's sharp voice pierced the air.

"We are in the bedroom," I hollered.

"I will be in the living room."

"Okay. We will join you in a minute."

. . .

Mama was seated on one of the Adirondack styled rattan chairs, her back erect, her thighs hugging each other, her glasses resting on the bridge of her nose. Her newly braided hair complemented her beautiful face. She was eating a guava. I walked to her, touched her feet and kissed her on her forehead. Mika kissed her on her cheeks. I took the guava from her and bit a mouthful. Mika looked at me. I touched the guava to her lips, rubbed it playfully over them. Smiling, she slapped my wrist and bit a chunk of the guava. I handed the rest to Mama. Mika remained standing beside Mama. I sat on the bench chair facing them, my feet resting on the edge of the trunk-coffee table.

"Mama, this is such lovely braiding," Mika said, kneeling beside Mama, fingering strands of her braided hair. "Very relaxed, not stiff at all . . ." lifting a handful, running it between her fingers, "nicely weaved . . . really lovely, compliments your fine features . . ."

"Thank you, dear. Such kind words," Mama said, smiling.

The two great loves of my life, cordial; supportive . . . perhaps I should leave them alone awhile.

"I will be in my study," I said, getting up.

"Stay. I must speak with you about last night. We were worried after Tòkunbò telephoned you several times with no answer. What happened, eh?" "Mama, you wouldn't believe it," Mika said.

"What happened?" Mama faced Mika who was still on her knees beside her.

"Angel . . ." Mika said looking at me.

Mama turned facing me. "Are you okay? Armed robbers attacked you?"

"No. One of these days, maybe," I said.

"Stop talking like that. Do not call evil on yourself. The wind has ears. Evil spirits are all over the place. I warn you not to speak like that but you do not listen to me," Mama said.

"Sorry," I said.

"So what happened? You had an emergency assignment to cover?"

"No."

Mika got up from her kneeling position beside Mama, walked over to me and sat next to me as I recounted my meeting and conversation with the General.

"That is very strange," Mama said.

"Maybe he is experiencing a change of heart," I said.

Mama stared into space.

"It is possible," she now said.

I nodded.

"Well, we just have to pray about it, leave it in God's hands . . . Maybe I should go to the village prophet to do consultation for you."

"He wants to see me again, so let's wait to see how it goes."

"I will pray for you. No danger will befall you."

"Thank you," I said, walked to her, touched her feet and kissed her on her forehead. She held my hand, gazed into my eyes.

"I will be okay," I said.

She smiled, feebly.

. . .

We lived joyfully the rest of the weekend. Mika and me spent time love dancing. (It is utter pleasure, a fulfilling hard work having for a partner an intelligent and beautiful woman blessed with a robust appetite for sex.) Mika worked on her garden, weeding it here and there, watering the flowers and plants. We both read and wrote, listened to music, particularly some of the "folk" music I have been collecting during my travels. At some point in our listening session Mika declared she would like to hear the sacred choral music of Bach. "Which one?" I said. She stared into space awhile. "Choose," she said. I decided on "*Komm heiliger Geist*"—Come Holy Spirit. (Of the music Mika had brought with her from Amsterdam, besides the music of Bach, I have come to cherish the music of Beethoven, Stravinsky and Manuel de Falla.) "Thank you, Angel," she said, resting her cheek on my heart as we both, in the dead of night, journeyed on the wings of Music into Bach's musical-religious universe, our bedroom in darkness but for the flickering yellowish light of the palm oil lamp. . . .

I spent time with Mama in her room. She told me she was convinced there were things going on in the world human beings were not aware of; that there was an underlying logic to Existence, which is why it was important that people remained with hope; that there was a purpose for each human being to fulfill in this life. She spoke about her father, as she often did. She told me she sometimes felt his presence about her, especially late at night; that he had appeared to her many times after his death, always smiling each time he did so; that she would wake up each time feeling all will be well with us. I told her, as I had done many times, I regretted he was no longer with us; that I missed him so much, and, recalling his comment to me years ago regarding a certain prophecy about me coming to pass, asked her if he ever said anything to her about me while I was in New York, before he died. "Apart from what I told you that just before he passed he told me to tell you goodbye, that your path is clear, that he is proud of you?" I nodded. "No," she said. "Is there something in particular you think he should have said?" Recalling his request that I should not tell Mama he said that to me, "No. Nothing in particular," I said.

At dawn on Monday I returned to the city.

## My Mother Whimpering on the Bed of History

Throughout that week the General was on my mind often. Was he in fact undergoing a transformation? Should I trust and encourage his friendliness with me? So cautious I was, so excited. I found myself wondering how the whole thing was going to unfold. If he was indeed on the verge of a moral transformation, what should my role be in helping him successfully achieve his moral re-birth? And what would this mean for the wellbeing of our people? . . .

On the night of the Thursday of that week, exactly a week after our first meeting, the General again sent Ibrahim and his men to fetch me.

Ibrahim again blindfolded me, used "sir" to address me, treated me courteously telling me "Mind your head, sir" as I got into the Mercedes-Benz. The driver made numerous abrupt stops and turns as he had done the last time, again frustrating my attempt to mentally map the route we were traveling. They took me to the same location. The General again let us in through the glass-door, which he opened by punching numbers on the remote control. He was seated on the imposing sofa puffing on a cigar, his fleshy arm resting on a shoulder of the sofa. He looked noble in a blue silk agbádá with brown embroidery at the neck, wrists and ankles. Ibrahim searched me in front of him. The only articles he found on me were my wallet and keys. The General promptly dismissed Ibrahim, and let in his white-uniformed servant, the same man as the last time. The servant performed his routine of eating and drinking just like the last time; the General intently watched him the whole time he did so. He then poured the General a drink, bowing as he handed it to him. He poured another drink and bowing handed it to me. Then, he stood in front of the General, his head bent. The General gently waved his hand thereby dismissing him, and pressed some numbers on the remote control. The door slid open. He exited the room. The General again pressed some numbers, the door slid shut behind him. True to his word the General had changed the combination for opening and closing the door.

My conversation with the General began with him thanking me for coming. I nodded. And for my "good" work with the Center. I again nodded. He asked me about the welfare of my family. I told him all is well with them. He asked me if I had kept my word to him regarding not telling anyone about our last meeting and conversation. I nodded, and immediately changed my mind deciding to tell him the truth. "Actually, I told Mama, and my woman, Mika. I can assure you they will absolutely keep it to themselves," I said. His middlefinger poking his temple, he gazed at me, smoke swirling above his head. "I thank you for telling me the truth," he said. I nodded. He puffed on his cigar.

"You did not want to talk about it the last time, but I am still interested in your opinion on what you think is wrong with our country," he said.

Silent, I looked him in the eyes, drank some cognac.

"I see you do not want to say anything to me . . . You do not trust my intentions . . ." He gazed at me.

"Can you blame me?" I maintained his gaze.

"I understand that you are being cautious. But how can you fail to see that I like you, eh? . . . I bring you here to my hideout . . ."

"Why? Tell me why? Convince me that your intentions are genuine," I interrupted him.

"You are like a young star. You carry such intense energy inside you."

"It is a good thing I am not inclined to violence."

He smiled, puffed on his cigar.

"As I was saying before you flared, you yourself know my reputation. You know that I am not usually accessible to people. I cannot trust anyone fully. Not even my friends. They all have daggers, waiting for an opportunity to plunge it in. Even the Brutus among them will be persuaded to go along when the time comes to stab me. And the intellectuals, journalists, all men of letters, you know how I am with them . . ."

"Oh, I know." I again interrupted him.

He ignored my comment.

"But you . . . I am drawn to you . . . your aura, your

spirit . . . I appreciate your love for our people, your effort in helping them through the wonderful work you are doing for their wellbeing through the Center . . ."

"But your Excellency, you could have done the same."

"Yes. But would that really solve our problem?"

"At the very least it would help our people a bit."

He gazed at me awhile, and then puffed on his cigar.

"As I was saying, I appreciate your effort. And your mind . . . your mind fascinates me. Although in your writings you make references to aspects of the life of our people, and the shortcomings of my government, I truly respect that you do not point fingers at anyone. I appreciate that your thought is mostly abstract, fundamental. You seek to get at the heart of the matter, unlike the others who call themselves intellectuals, but who merely babble, point fingers, name names . . ."

"Your Excellency, I am flattered . . ."

"No need to be flattered. I am telling the truth. God is my witness . . . you make me want to do something . . . I know that I have been bad all these years. It has not been easy on my conscience, believe me. And lately, my conscience bothers me for the bad things I have done . . . In my private moments, there is not a time that I do not feel guilt for my conduct all these years . . . so I smoke, puffing non-stop like a chimney . . . I drink . . . I indulge in narcotics, in sex. I am oversexed . . . not good for a man's inner spirit. I do all these to placate my guilty conscience . . . to forget myself . . . to forget my immoral actions . . . Nowadays, I am tormented with the need to atone, and a voice deep inside me tells me that you are important to my repentance. Since I first set my eyes on you when you were introduced to me at the State House, about to start covering my government, I have had this feeling, a strong feeling of an opportunity, a once in a lifetime opportunity, to make amends for my evil deeds, for my sins. That is why I am so irresistibly drawn to you . . ." He puffed on his cigar, the smoke veiling the remorse dulling his usually bright, bulging eyes. "You should know what talking to you like this means to me . . ." he continued, "I am a proud man. But you, you humble me, you make me want to do something . . ." He stared at me. "I have said enough. If you do not want to talk, that is all right. I have extended my hand in friendship. Take it if you want. But know this," he waggled his chubby middlefinger at me, "I will show you that I mean well."

When he commented about his being 'oversexed', saying it is not good for a man's inner spirit, I wanted to interrupt him, to say I disagree, that, perhaps, the opposite is true of sex. I had not done so because I was so enchanted by his earnest revelation of himself. Everything about his demeanor just then impressed me as genuine, and I was becoming convinced of his good intentions. I was touched by what he said about himself, and decided not to question him on what he meant by "I will show you that I mean well."

Since Africa visited me in New York I had banished my reason to a cage deep inside me and only consulted it from time to time. I never allowed it to fully influence my decisions. Seated there in front of the General, I opened the door to the cage and consulted my reason. Its advice, of course, was: *"Be cautious. You are dealing with a dictator with a long history of brutality, especially to your kind."* My intuition: *"Nothing to fear. Listen to your heart."* At that moment I recalled what Africa had told me: *"You must conquer fear. Nothing will happen to you that is not fated."*

"I thank you for sharing your private thoughts with me, your Excellency. And I believe you mean well with me. I hope you appreciate my being cautious," I said.

He sat gazing at me.

I drank some cognac.

A smile now began crawling on his face, causing the corners of his mouth to twitch. Still gazing at me he puffed repeatedly on his cigar, smoke swirling round his face, waltzing above his head.

I again drank some cognac. As I replaced the goblet onto the coffee table I noticed he was staring into space, his eyes squinted.

"Your Excellency, I am curious . . . do you like Literature?" He shifted on the sofa, uncrossed his legs, folded his exquisite agbádá onto his lap and re-crossed his legs. "I ask only because of your earlier reference to *Julius Caesar*," I said.

"Yes I did mention Brutus . . ." He puffed on his cigar. "Òdodo, I hope you are not one of those people who think dictators, so called, are ignorant bastards . . . maybe some are, but not this one," he tapped his chest, "I am an educated man, relatively anyway . . . not well read like you . . . far from it. We military men, we spend the majority of our training in military academies, but I do read books even though not as much as I should . . . And I am able to remember a great deal. A dictator cannot survive without a good memory. He must spend all his mental energy on remembering. I have what they call a photographic memory. I am able to remember entire conversations, books . . . Yes, I do read books. I have read *Julius Caesar* . . . *The Prince* . . . I have *The Prince* entirely in my head." He tapped his temple with his fingertip. "I have learned a great deal from books. Machiavelli speaks directly to me when he says . . ." He squinted as he tried to recollect what it was he wanted to say. "Ah, yes . . . when he says: 'He who establishes a dictatorship and does not kill Brutus, or he who founds a republic and does not kill the sons of Brutus, will only reign a short time.'"

"You are familiar with Machiavelli's other works," I said, surprised by his reference to *The Discourses*. "That is interesting, your Excellency."

"I know *The Discourses* very well. I have a copy of it."

"You do?"

Smiling, he nodded.

"Your Excellency, I must admit that I am impressed. One would never have guessed that you read Literature, and keenly," I, smiling, said, betraying my pleasure. If you seek a passage to my heart, talk about Literature, talk about ideas. The General had my attention.

"I know what you mean . . . a dictator is supposed to be an ignorant fool. That is one of the biggest lies in the world . . . A dictator is a cunning character with an acute insight into human motivation. He understands that the best way to maintain his power is to create an atmosphere of fear that perpetuates his domination because the majority will be afraid to challenge him. The fearless intellectuals and the university students, he must necessarily suppress by brutalizing them. As for himself, the dictator must meticulously cultivate an enigmatic personality . . . people must be kept guessing, perpetually unsure. The dictator also necessarily realizes the need to create a web of patronage to support himself . . . He craves and in fact needs total control because he is constantly tormented by a feeling of insecurity and only his ability to exercise absolute power gives him the feeling of control . . . Besides, the dictator craves absolute power because he is compelled to do so in order to maintain his position. And because he constantly feels that his security is threatened, he resorts to cruelty even against his own morals and better judgment . . . brutality becomes for him a matter of absolute necessity to stay alive, he surrounds himself with an army of security agents . . ." He puffed on his cigar.

I was impressed with his astute analysis of the psyche of a dictator.

"That was quite eloquent, your Excellency . . . of course I do not mean to suggest that you are incapable of such knowledge . . . I do not mean to suggest that you are incapable of such a brilliant analysis of the inner world of a dictator."

"Ah," he waved his hand in the air, "do not worry. I like you. I am sure you know that by now . . . you know, eh?" He smiled.

I nodded, smiled also.

"Good. I want to assure you that you are not in danger at all. So, speak with me freely."

"Thank you, your Excellency."

"No need to say that, Òdodo . . . no need at all," he, again smiling, said his laugh-lines boldly stretched round his mouth.

"Well, as I am sure you know, your Excellency, I am in a lifelong devotion to Knowledge. I read a lot. I like to say that I am a career student . . . And there is my profession, which, of course, requires that I read." He nodded. "Your Excellency, I am sure you know that Literature can impart knowledge about Existence."

"That is true, very true indeed, but what if the person does not know exactly which books to read . . ."

His comment excited me. And I had an idea then of how things might unfold between us.

"That is not a problem if one has a friend who is relatively well read." "True," he said nodding, and stared into space, intermittently puffing on his cigar.

"I was just now thinking about names, your Excellency."

"What about them?"

"Given that my name means Truth . . ."

"It also means flower." He smiled.

"True. But with different accents on the vowels."

"I should have known you are too bright to let me win that."

We both smiled.

"As I was saying, given that my name means Truth I believe my interest in Literature, my pursuit of Knowledge are inevitable . . . I feel that it is my destiny to lust for Knowledge. I am sure you know the belief of our people that names are suggestive of the destiny of the bearer."

"I see what you mean."

"You assured me I could speak freely . . ."

"Yes, please. Speak your mind." He smiled "I am sure you have noticed that this is a soundproofed room. That monitor," he pointed to it on the floor across the room, "watches the entire building, certain parts of it in particular."

"I see the blinking light at its base, but it is not on . . ."

"You say that because you do not know its mechanism." He smiled.

"I see," I said.

"As I was saying, our conversation is private, completely private." He gazed at me. "Òdodo, believe me, this is the most relaxed I have been in a long time. I am used to playing roles but now, this moment," he jabbed his forefinger downward, "I am me." He tapped his chest with his forefinger.

"I am happy to hear that, your Excellency. And as I was saying, I have often thought about the fact that your behavior contradicts your name."

"I sensed this would be your comment when you mentioned names and destiny . . . I have often thought about the contradiction myself . . . I think about it a lot lately."

"Your Excellency, you have been doing some soul searching lately?"

"Don't psychoanalyze me. Not yet, anyway. Why rush, eh?" He smiled. "We are going to spend a lot more time together. This is just the beginning."

"I would love that very much, your Excellency. I look forward to it."

"Good, good."

"As I was saying before I turned a psychoanalyst . . ." His soft laughter interrupted me.

He puffed on his cigar, tilted his head backwards, exhaled smoke toward the ceiling and rearranged himself on the sofa.

"That was good. I like your sense of humor. I will tell you a secret: I enjoy humor a lot. But in my position, one cannot afford to joke around. It will be interpreted as a sign of being soft. So a man like me must be serious at all times."

"That line about my psychoanalyzing you too soon clearly shows your sense of humor, your Excellency."

"It is a rare occasion. I must take full advantage of it."

He puffed some more on his cigar, and stared into space. I drank the rest of my cognac.

"More drink, your Excellency?"

"Yes, thank you."

I poured some more drink into both our goblets.

"You were talking about books," he said.

"Oh, yes . . . I read on many subjects. I actually read International Relations for my Bachelors. And I am very much interested in political philosophies . . ."

"I know," he said, smiling.

"How?"

"I had you investigated."

"Really?"

"Do not worry. It is a standard thing for me to do."

"Your Excellency, you should tell me about me. Maybe you know me better than I know myself." I smiled.

"Well what do you want to know?" He smiled.

"Everything you know about me, your Excellency."

"Let me put it this way, I knew about you since you started writing in New York. And I know enough about you now to know that you are the right person to reach out to . . . I know that you will be my salvation . . . Please do not ask me for an explanation . . ."

"I am a patient person, your Excellency. I promise not to pester you on anything. Whatever you wish me to know, you will tell me whenever you choose."

"The intellect you displayed with your response just now, your grace . . . and the help you are giving our people are why I admire you so much."

"Thank you, your Excellency. You are so kind with your words."

"I should be thanking you."

I was not sure what to make of his comment that he should be thanking me.

"As I was saying about books, these days I read mostly fiction . . . novels, poems, plays . . . and I read essays, biographies, philosophy . . ."

"I do not read novels or poems at all, never have . . . but I have read *Julius Caesar* . . . it was given to me by an acquaintance because of what it teaches rulers. She also gave me *The Prince*. You cannot imagine how important that book has been to me all these years . . . Until recently, I slept with it on my nightstand and I often read passages from it. In fact, I re-read the entire book periodically."

I thought about his comment, thinking fascinating, to say the least, the ironic duality that often characterizes Literature. Machiavelli wrote *The Prince* as a contribution to knowledge about, you might say, social psychology; here was a dictator using it (rightly?) as a manual for dominating his people.

"Your Excellency, you will enjoy novels, trust me. For

one thing, I think it would be good for you to read the works of African novelists. You wanted to know my opinion on the country's situation . . . I would suggest that you read the work of African novelists which deal with the social reality here in Africa . . . Regarding the miserable existence of the majority of our people, you cannot imagine how progressive are many of the ideas we have right here in Africa . . . ideas that if utilized would transform Africa from Cape Town to Cairo . . . many Africans both here on the continent and overseas have been thinking deeply about the wellbeing of Africa . . ."

Silent, he sat gazing at me.

"And beyond issues specific to Africa, our novelists also explore issues concerning human beings generally. As I am sure you know we have some widely recognized writers."

He nodded.

"And there are great European, Asian, North and South American novelists, novelists worthy of the designation, insightful writers, devoted thinkers . . . their work is pregnant with profound ideas."

Silent, he kept gazing at me.

"And there are works of political philosophy I think you should read."

"Do you always get this excited when you talk about books? You are gesticulating like an impassioned preacher." He smiled.

He was right. I had all along been waving my arm about, jabbing the air with my fingers.

"I am my mother's child. I got it from her. You should see her discuss with me."

He laughed, puffed on his cigar and stared into space.

"I am thinking . . . I would like to give you an assignment. I want you to prepare for me a list of important books you think I ought to read . . . At this point in my life I am most interested in books on metaphysics, philosophy, political theory, economic theory, sociology, history . . . I hope your list would include books on these. And you just mentioned novels . . . give me some African novels you like . . . I want to know what they are saying about life, about Africa . . . you are right, their words may be good . . . one may find wisdom in it," he now said.

"I believe you will, your Excellency. That is why I have long thought that our leaders should read the work of our writers and learn from it instead of throwing them in jail or chasing them away to foreign lands. I assure you there is vision in their work, vivid visions of the possibilities for our progress."

"I want to read them . . . know firsthand what you are saying about them."

"Your Excellency, I am very happy you want me to do this . . . Literature makes us conscious of the world, and that is very important because an unconscious person might as well be dead."

He nodded, repeatedly.

"As I said earlier, we military men are not well read. We are trained to defend the status quo. To deal with people who are deemed dangerous to it." He puffed on his cigar, drank and stared into space holding the goblet. He now gazed at me. "That is hardly the kind of education to impart the consciousness you have in mind . . . I take it you mean awareness of why things are the way they are in the world?"

"I am happy you recognized my use of the word. Thank you."

"My pleasure, Òdodo, my pleasure."

"The good thing about a book is that one can pick it up anytime."

"You are right about that . . . and we could not have been having this conversation at a better time because the time has really come for me to spread Knowledge in a way that men would understand."

I smiled.

"You like what I just said, eh?"

"Yes, very much. And I am curious to know why you want to do this, and why now, your Excellency."

"In due time, Òdodo . . . in due time you will know."

He sat puffing on his cigar, staring into space.

I drank some cognac.

"We have hardly touched the peas. They are from Japan, soy-roasted, very good, goes nicely with the cognac, I must say," he now said, scooping a handful.

"The mouth has been busy, your Excellency. Such good conversation we are having. And I agree, the peas are tasty," I scooped a handful, tossed them in my cupped palms, "although I should point out that we have peanuts right here in Africa."

"I recognize that idea in some of your articles. You would like to see more commerce among African countries."

"Not that we should neglect trade with the rest of the world. But, yes, more commerce is needed amongst ourselves," I said, clarifying my thoughts in the pieces he referred to.

"I understand," he said.

"More economic intercourse amongst ourselves is one sure way to ensure a better economic future for Africa . . . I hope the day will come when one can take a train from Tangier directly to Lagos, and all the way down to Cape Town . . . Felá said it well in his song, 'Buy Africa'."

"You like him, eh?"

"Yes. I appreciate him for his fearless spirit, for his love for Africa, for dedicating his life to the struggle for the progress of our people."

"God knows that those of us in high places in government all over Africa like him too. But we cannot show that publicly . . . Yes, Felá was a fearless soldier for Freedom . . . there will never be another like him."

"I second that opinion, your Excellency."

"Speaking of Japanese nuts, maybe we should keep buying them," I said, smiling. "My woman, Mika, she is partly Japanese, partly Ghanaian and Zimbabwean."

He started to smile.

"You probably know that too."

"Actually, I do."

"I am not surprised at all."

"I had to do my homework on you. She is a beautiful woman, I must say. You are a lucky man."

"Thank you, your Excellency. She is special, really . . . intelligent, has a communal heart . . . a man cannot wish for a better woman."

"I would like to meet her. And your mother too."

"It would be my pleasure to introduce you to them, your Excellency." "Good, good. So when do you think you will have the books ready?"

"Oh, not long at all. A week . . ."

"Good, good."

"Your Excellency, I do not know how to get them to you."

"I will send my men to get them. My men, they have not been rude to you, they have not disrespected you in any way, eh?"

"Oh, not at all. In fact, Ibrahim has been so courteous."

"Good, good. Next Thursday, I will send Ibrahim. That will give you a week. I hope that is enough time."

"That is plenty of time. I will begin assembling them tonight," I said, downing the rest of my drink in one gulp. "Your Excellency, thank you for a very good evening."

"Thank you for coming," he said shaking my hand, his palm silky. He held on to my hand, looked into my eyes. "Thank you for warming up to me," he said.

"My pleasure, your Excellency. I am glad that I did."

The General pressed some numbers on the remote; Ibrahim's face instantly appeared on the monitor. The General watched him walk toward the door and pressed the combination when he neared it. The door slid open. Ibrahim entered the room. "Your Excellency," he said, bowed. The General looked at him. He again bowed. The General smiled at me as I followed Ibrahim into the corridor.

. . .

I lay on my bed recalling my meeting with the General, excited at the possibility to affect his thoughts, his actions. My excitement was soon lessened by the devilish voice of Reason in my head: *"Be cautious, you are dealing with a cunning dictator."* Intuition counseled: *"Follow your heart. There is nothing to fear."* . . . I lay on the bed recalling my meeting with the General, drowsy.

. . .

I now notice the pregnant moon gazing at my bedroom through the open window. As I now feel an eerie atmosphere about me, I turn my gaze from the moon. She is seated on the edge of my bed. Tall and long limbed; her jet black skin lustrous. She is wearing the same white linen dress she wore when she appeared to me in New York, bejeweled in gold and diamond. She smells sweet, but for a whiff of oil.

She sits gazing at me. I sit up in bed; rest my back against the wall. Smiling, gazing at me, her ethereal looking eyes luminous, she moves closer to me.

"My dear child," she says in her odd nasal voice, stroking my cheek, her touch feathery, cold, "I told you I would appear to you when you need me and when I need you. I am here to talk to you about Jéjélayé."

Silent, I sit wondering what it was she wanted to say about the General.

"He is undergoing a change of heart. You, my dear child, have a purpose to fulfill in his life. Open your heart to him. There is nothing to fear, you hear?"

I nod.

"You must always remember that nothing will happen to you that is not fated. You understand?"

I again nod.

"Good, my dear child, good."

"When you came to me in New York, I had . . ."

"You had questions you wanted to ask me but you were too awed by me to ask them then." She interrupts me. "So you would like to ask them now."

"Yes. I would like to ask you some questions."

"I will hear them."

"In New York, you spoke of your abuse at the hands of both your children, and foreigners. I had wanted very much to ask you to explain that to me . . . of course I know generally what you mean, but I want you to tell me precisely . . . I want you to fully explain to me how and why they do it . . . I want to comprehend your agonizing existence, your bondage so that I will know for sure how best to work for your liberation . . ."

Silent, she sits gazing at me.

"My dear child, I will answer your question by showing you something. Bring me some cool water in a white bowl," she now says. "And a white linen."

"Water in a white bowl, and white linen," I mutter to myself getting up from the bed. She remains seated on the edge of the bed.

Now back in the room I see Her standing in front of the window smiling at the moon.

"Is this okay?" I say showing her one of my white linen wrappers.

"Yes. It will do," she says without looking at it.

She now turns round, takes the wrapper from me and spreads it on the floor. She sits on one side of it, crosses Her lean long legs under Her and straightens Her back. She takes the bowl of water from me and places it before Her.

"Sit down there." She points to the spot directly opposite Her. I sit, cross my legs under me grateful Mika had taught and encouraged me to sit so. She smiles at me. Silent, we remain seated cross legged on the wrapper, the bowl of water between us, a distant look in Her eyes. She now begins to trace the rim of the bowl with the tip of Her left middlefinger, repeatedly. Now presses both Her palms on the sides of the bowl, closes Her eyes, leans forward and hunches over the bowl covering it with Her torso. She remains in the position, mumbling unintelligibly. Her eyes still closed, she now slowly leans back from the bowl, sits erect, opens Her eyes and gazes into mine. Again mumbling unintelligibly, she simultaneously places Her middlefinger on the center of my skull and Her thumb on the center of my forehead, pressing hard on them. Still mumbling, gazing into my eyes, she starts to close and open her eyes repeatedly. I realize she is motioning me to close my eyes. I feel Her feathery hand on my face, on my closed eyes. With the tip of Her thumb and middlefinger she begins to rub both my closed eyes in a circular motion, slowly, repeatedly. "Look into the bowl," she now says. "My dear child, behold the Drama, my earthly reality." She gently pushes the bowl of water toward me.

In the water I see Africa dressed in Her immaculate

linen dress and bejeweled as usual. She stands looking at some of Her children tending a herd of muscled cattle whose wide and long horns point to the heavens. Her hands on Her sculptured hip, Her star eyes thinned by a wide smile, Her teeth like sun bleached elephant tusk, she holds a gold and ivory pipe at the corner of Her mouth, smoke from it curling in front of Her face. . . .

In the distance I see a camel, a cloud of dust whirling behind it. The face of its rider is framed by a voluminous beige turban, wearing an ankle length beige caftan, a scimitar hanging from his waist, his blazing eyes focused ahead of him in the direction of Africa. More camels appear behind him. Their riders are dressed as their leader. . . .

It is now impossible to see anything because the scene is unfolding at a dizzying, blinding speed.

I raise my head from the bowl and stare at Africa seated motionless in front of me, Her legs crossed under Her like the Buddha.

"Look in the bowl," she says.

"I can no longer see anything. The speed . . ."

"The divine speed. Look now." She interrupts me.

I look in the bowl.

The scene has changed. Africa is now seated on a mat woven of bamboo leaves under an ìrókò tree whose protruding veins snaked the ground about it. A dark-skinned and wooly haired boy is fanning Her with a deep-green banana leaf, big like the ear of an adult bull-elephant. Not far from where she sits, the ocean is wailing, roaring, hurling herself at the shore, lashing at the mounds of sand sprawled at her feet restraining her from rushing inland, folding and unfolding her waves of liquid-cloth, frothy in the mouth like a grieving woman whose baby has been yanked from her by an invading army and is left angered and distressed, tying and untying her wrapper, tearing at her hair, lashing at those restraining her from flinging herself on the ground as she grieves for the certain fate she knows is about to befall her child. . . .

A ship now appears on the ocean slowly approaching the shore . . .

It is again impossible to see anything because the scene is once more unfolding at a blinding speed . . .

"Keep looking," Africa says before I could raise my head from the bowl; she obviously knows when the scene fast-forwards.

The scene has again changed. I see a stage. In the center of it is a huge four-post wooden bed. On the headrest of the bed is engraved:

"There Is No God But Allah, And Mohammed Is His Messenger."

"Christ is the Light and the Way"

"Modernity: The Age of Reason."

The bed is covered with white linen. On the bed lay naked Africa, voluptuous.

Embarrassed to see Her naked I raise my head from the bowl and look at Her.

"Go on. Behold my earthly reality," she, smiling, says.

I look in the bowl.

On the bed lay Africa, naked, Her arms and legs tied to the long posts of the bed, Her white linen dress in a heap on the floor. Seated majestically on the floor by the posts of the bed are four lions, glowing sunset their eyes. Atop Africa is an incredibly tall, gorilla-looking being; his deep-seated eyes are intensely dark and luminous; his skin is somewhat scaly. Below Africa is another tall, leopard skinned being; he also has dark and luminous eyes; his head is small relative to his huge body and towering height. Some of the other huge beings on and around the bed look like felines, their slant eyes dark and luminous. Others have wings for hands, their noses shaped like the beak of a bird of prey. Still others look like men and women, some of them half human, half animal. One of them is partly hidden from my view. From the little I see of him, he looks familiar. Red and brown colors, bright and clear, are radiating from the bodies of all the beings. Africa lay on the bed sandwiched between the gorilla being and the leopard being. They both are vigorously penetrating Her, the one Her front, the other

Her behind, gyrating recklessly, grunting loudly, specks dotting their foreheads, rivulets of sweat snaking down their spines. Africa is writhing, whimpering. Some of the other beings are stroking Her, finger-penetrating Her in Her ears, Her armpits. Others are stroking Her arm, kissing Her toes, simultaneously finger-penetrating themselves, their eyes molten with pleasure. One of the feline-looking beings stands by a bedpost stroking his humongous, inhuman penis, another is finger-penetrating herself . . . Two beings dressed in white robes sit on the edge of the bed. The face of one of them is cleanly shaved, his straight silvery hair covered with a cap. The head of the other is totally shaved, but wearing a bushy gray sideburn, moustache and long beard. Red and brown colors, bright and clear, are radiating from their bodies. Each of them is holding a Book. They are passionately reading passages from their Book to Africa as she lays on the bed writhing and whimpering between the gorilla being and the leopard being, both of whom continue to vigorously penetrate Her, gyrating recklessly, grunting loudly, more specks dotting their foreheads, coalescing and snaking down their spines. Thick and shiny blackish blood is now seeping from between Africa's thighs; with the blood is coming out glittering yellow clots and sparkling spectrum-color clots. The beings scramble for the clots.

Some persons now appear. Some of them are clutching pens and notepads. Others are carrying guitar, banjo, woodwinds, trumpet, doussn'gouni, maraca, calabash, bells, kora, conga, talking drum, drum, accordion, mbira, zanza, marimba, organ, microphones and many other instruments for making music. Still others are carrying cameras. I am among them; Abdul is beside me. Some more persons appear. One of them, his eyebrows and mustache bushy, is holding a book titled "KING LEOPOLD'S SOLILOQUY." Another, a book, his photograph on its front cover, titled "WHY WE CAN'T WAIT." Still others are holding books:

THE SHADOW OF THE SUN
SOMETHING OUT THERE

THINGS FALL APART
TWO THOUSAND SEASONS
AN AFRICAN ELEGY
ASTONISHING THE GODS

MODERN AFRICA
THE OPEN SORE OF A CONTINENT
THE BLACK MAN'S BURDEN
LET FREEDOM COME: AFRICA IN MODERN HISTORY

Among them, a charming woman, smiling blissfully, is holding a book titled "THE POISONWOOD BIBLE," her photograph on its back cover. "Others are holding LPs, compact discs and videocassettes, their photographs on the covers of some of them:

IMMIGRANT SLAVE SONG
AFRICA TEARS AND LAUGHTER

NORTH AND SOUTH
GODS AND MEN
WHY CAN'T WE LIVE TOGETHER

OPPOSITE PEOPLE
CONFUSION
DOG EAT DOG
SORROW TEARS AND BLOOD
UNDERGROUND SYSTEM
ARMY ARRANGEMENT
NO AGREEMENT

UPRISING
BUFFALO SOLDIERS
BUSTIN' OUT OF TRENCHTOWN
THE TRANCE OF SEVEN COLORS

TERRESTRIAL BEINGS
FILLES DE KILIMANJARO
SEE-LINE WOMAN
TAR BABY
SANKOFA
NEW MOON DAUGHTER
FOUR WOMEN
BLACK, BROWN AND BEIGE
MULTIKULTI
STRANGE FRUIT
NAIMA
COUSIN MARY
INDIA
MR. P.C.
GUELWAAR
OTOMO
LUMUMBA
GET UP STAND UP
LET IT ALL OUT
THULASIZWE/I SHALL BE RELEASED!

LIVELY UP YOURSELF
REJOICE
MESSAGE FROM HOME
OUR ROOTS BEGAN IN AFRICA
HEAVEN'S HERE ON EARTH

EXODUS
TRAVELING MILES
MILES AHEAD
KIND OF BLUE
WALKIN'
IN A SILENT WAY

THE JUNGLE LINE
THE HISSING OF SUMMER LAWNS
ELECTRIC AFRICA
MONEY JUNGLE

CROSS ROADS
NEW BEGINNING

LIVE-EVIL
BITCHES BREW
YOU'RE UNDER ARREST

ONE LOVE / PEOPLE GET READY
GONDWANA
PANGAEA
RENAISSANCE
IT'S ABOUT THAT TIME

MILES SMILES

Many more Africans, and friends of Africa, friends of Man, appear and join us. Heads of shimmering blond hair, heads of flaming red hair and glossy brunette hair stand shoulder to shoulder with heads of lustrous and thick kinky and wooly hair. Radiating from our bodies are blue, yellow, green and white colors, some cloud like, others bright and clear. Here we all are, Jews and Gentiles; sons and daughters of the sky and of the earth; sons and daughters of the gods and of men; sons and daughters of the North and of the South, of the West and of the East. All of us march together toward the bed; many hands raised, fingers balled into fists; hands scribbling into notepads; eyes peering into viewfinders of cameras focused on the bed recording the domination of Africa; mouths open wide over microphones; drums thundering, woodwinds shrieking, mbiras and zanza vibrating, marimba and organs clanking. We are all wailing: THE HUMAN RACE IS NOT YET FREE. THE HUMAN RACE MUST BE FREED! WE WILL NEVER GIVE UP THE STRUGGLE. AND WE WILL OVERCOME.

DESTINY IS OUR FRIEND. The lions are snarling at us. The beings now pause from their scrambling for Africa's gem-clots, covering their humongous ears with the flat of their equally humongous hands. A man now appears. He is hurriedly setting up his camera, now peering into its viewfinder, recording the rape of Africa. On the forehead area of his blue bucket-hat is inscribed *NY* in yellow letters. On the chest area of his blue tee shirt is inscribed in yellow bold letters: THE END OF THE GAME. The gorilla being and the leopard being resume their position atop and below Africa and continue to penetrate Her. Some of the others also climb into bed and resume their fondling and poking of Her. The others crowd around the bed watching, some of them simultaneously fondling themselves, others finger-penetrating themselves. Felá now puts down his trumpet, someone hands him a saxophone. He moves closer to the bed, stands rigid by the side of the bed, begins to blow, the sound jarring, the nearby lion snarling at him. He begins blowing into an ear of the gorilla being, who, grunting, continues to penetrate Africa, his eyes closed. The gorilla being stops, turns to face Felá, his dark eyes luminous, growls at Felá, kicks him in the groin. Felá staggers, falls, hitting his head on the floor, his saxophone clattering against the floor. Felá grabs his groin, his face contorts with pain. He hoists himself up pressing his palm flat on the floor, picks up his saxophone, walks back to the side of the bed sucking on his lower lip. He resumes blowing into the ear of the gorilla being who is back at his position atop Africa, vigorously humping Her. Felá is blowing louder. All the other music makers are also singing and playing louder, the lions snarling at them, their incisors like miniature elephant tusks. The music makers continue playing, the sound gloriously loud. The rest of us continue wailing: THE HUMAN RACE MUST BE FREED! The person holding the book titled ASTONISHING THE GODS continues to serenely scribble in his notepad as he wails. The beings, again covering their ears with their palms, begin growling, hissing, yapping, red and brown colors radiating from their bodies. . . .

I now clearly see the being I saw earlier, who had been partly hidden from my view. Naked, he is walking backwards from the bed, gazing at me as I wail, remorse seated heavily in his big eyes. He continues to back away from the bed, tears snaking down his fleshy cheeks. There is a door behind him, on the ledge of which is seated an eagle. He continues to back away toward the door. . . .

I raise my head from the bowl and wipe the tears wriggling down my cheeks with the back of my hand. I again look into the bowl. My reflection in the water stares back at me.

I raise my head and stare at Africa seated in front of me.

"That is enough," she says.

"What do you mean enough? Why did you stop it?"

"Do not raise your voice at me. You hear?"

"Why did you stop it?" I say louder.

"You have seen enough of the Drama. That is all you need to know of my earthly reality."

"I saw General Jéjélayé. He was walking away from the stage. Let me see the rest . . . please."

"No. That is all I will show you. The rest of it will be too painful. You are already crying from the little you saw."

"I want to see."

"No. That is enough. The rest of it will be too weighty for you. You already have a Cross to bear as it is."

"Right now, I do not care about that. I want to see the rest of what is happening on the stage. I want to see what Jéjélayé does. I want to see the rest of the Drama. I want to know its conclusion."

"Believe me, my dear son. What you have seen is enough.

"This is crazy. Why are some of your own children among those abusing you? And Jéjélayé. He is . . ."

"Remember what I told you about his ongoing change of heart?" She interrupts me.

I nod.

"There is a purpose for you to fulfill in his life. Both your destinies are linked. He needs you now. And I need you both."

"But how come our destinies are linked? I am a journalist devoted to Truth. Jéjélayé is a dictator, the most powerful man in the land. He thrives on lies, the inculcation of fear. His wish is law. How can my destiny be linked with that of a man like him?"

"Òdodo, you are thinking with only your head, like a man . . ."

"How else am I supposed to think? Like a god?"

She smiles.

"Òdodo, you should not think as mortals do. Mortals have taken to thinking about everything by mostly using their ability to reason. They have become slaves of Reason, crowned It their King, institutionalized It as the Guide of their life, made It their God. Reason now sits on their breasts, informing and influencing their thoughts and deeds . . . You are thinking like a mortal. That is why you made that comment about the difference between you and Jéjélayé. As I told you in New York, Reason is both the Light and Darkness of mortals. You must be wary of Reason. If you must listen to Reason, do so with Heart."

She is contradicting Herself. How could one listen to one's head through one's heart?

"You are thinking again. Stop thinking about what I am saying to you. Listen to me with your heart, you hear?"

I nod.

"My dear child, what you must know is that everything happens on a psychic level. You must think of things in a spiritual sense. And you can do that. You hear?" she says loudly, her voice nasal. "You have more power than you realize. As I said earlier, you are a messenger."

"You must fully explain that."

"No explanation is needed. In due time, you will come to comprehend all I am saying to you. What you need to know now is that you must stay with Jéjélayé. Your destinies are linked. You need each other. I need you both. That is all I will say on the matter."

"What is your secret, anyway? You just showed me yourself being molested, whimpering in agony. And here you are in front of me seated serenely . . . And why do you physically resemble Mika? Why are you in her body? I have noticed your resemblance to her since New York. Tell me why you are in my woman's body. You are long limbed just like her . . . your graceful long neck, your narrow eyes, your high cheek bones, your alluring lips, your erect breasts crowned with proud nipples." She smiled. "I wish you were not so beautiful, not so rich, not so radiant . . . your sensuousness, your gold earrings, your huge diamond pendant, your sunny existence . . . maybe you should not so gallantly display your wealth . . . maybe then they will leave you alone, have no need to be falling over themselves scrambling for your riches . . . I wish your reality were different . . . that you were some poor, ugly, cold woman . . . that way you would be left alone."

She again smiles. Why does she keep smiling? How baffling.

"How precious you are, Òdodo." She gazes into my eyes. "I appreciate your concern about my abuse. But you must not think of me as you do mortals. I am Immortal. A Spirit. I can manifest in mortal form as I am appearing to you now, as I am in that scene, tied to the bed of History in the Drama of Life. In that scene, on that bed, it is my body they are assaulting. It is my flesh they are feasting on. What is most important is my spirit, my essence. It is alive and must remain so . . . Òdodo, my dear child." She strokes my cheeks. "Everything happens on a psychic level. You must always remember that. As long as my spirit remains alive, there is hope of my emancipation. If and when they annihilate my spirit, my true essence, that will be the end of me. But fear not, it will never happen. From the beginning, besides their assault of my flesh, they have endeavored to capture my spirit, but they have failed. And they will continue to fail. Although my spirit is not as wholesome as it used to be, it will never die. I will never capitulate. And in time my body will be freed. With loyal children like yourself joining the struggle for my freedom alongside your brothers and sisters, brave on the stage of History, Felá wailing with his saxophone, my wise son of letters recording everything diligently, in coded language for my living and yet unborn visionary children scattered all over the world, who will one day comprehend and come to know what to do to fully liberate me. With a new generation of loyal children like you, and my sympathizers, agents of Freedom all over the world, my spirit will never be annihilated, and in time my body too will be freed. Whatever I have lost will be regained fully. Whatever blemishes are left on my body will be cleansed. My glory will be restored. As I desire it so shall it be! It is with my liberation, with the full restoration of my glory and with the attainment of freedom for all my children all over the world that the Drama of Life will end, and then begin again." She gazes into my eyes. "You understand?"

I nod.

"What I have just told you goes beyond my own earthly reality. It is everything you need to know about Existence. You understand?"

I again nod.

"You must think cosmically."

"I do."

"I know. But I must remind you." She smiles. "And, as for your woman, you should know that I can take any shape I desire."

"But why that of Mika?"

"I do not exactly resemble Mika. I am dark. Her hue is that of amber."

"I appreciate your knack for poetic language, but you know that I am right. Physically you look like Mika. You have the same bone structure and features, so the slight difference in your skin color does not matter."

She smiles.

"I will tell you only this: Mika's destiny is linked with mine. And my destiny, Mika's destiny, your destiny and Jéjélayé's destiny are all interconnected."

"Please explain that."

"No explanation is needed. As I have told you, you cannot escape your destiny. Your earthly reality, from the moment you were born, your friends, and all the people you have met, you have met them all for a purpose. You, Mika, Abdul, Jéjélayé, and all those you saw on the stage of History struggling to liberate me, all of you are messengers of Love, Spirits in Flesh. That is why all of you are strong-willed, introspective and hate domination. That is why your innermost desire is to fight for my liberation, for the liberation and wellbeing of all my children all over the world, for the liberation and wellbeing of all dominated people because the struggle is not for only my liberation but for the liberation of all dominated people. Universal Love, Universal Freedom is the goal. It is hard to realize. It is with its realization that the world will end, and then begin again . . . Stay with Jéjélayé, open your heart to him. Your destinies are linked. My destiny is linked to both of yours. I need you both. You hear?"

I nod.

"Good, my child, good." She strokes my cheek. "Bring me a glass of water. My throat is dry from talking so much."

I go into the kitchen.

Now back in the bedroom balancing a jug of cold water in my right palm and a small bowl of fruit-salad I had brought for her in my left. I stand looking at the empty spot where she had sat. I smile, thinking how clever of Her to have sent me to fetch Her some water. She probably knew I would go on bombarding her with questions.

. . .

The intense gaze of the sun through my open bedroom window roused me early the next morning. A cup of Kenyan coffee fully woke me. I finished an article I had been working on. Then with Miles in the background playing "In A Silent Way/It's About That Time", I mused on my meetings with the General and wrote some notes in my journal. Later that afternoon I left the bungalow and drove to Freedom House.

I found Mama hunched over her sewing machine, her feet pressing on its pedal, her glasses perched on the bridge of her nose, her eyes focused on the long needle speedily perforating the edge of a linen fabric she was sewing into a dress for one of the villagers, a tape-measure loosely wrapped round her neck, her radio droning in the background.

"Mama."

She moved her chair from the sewing machine and

turned to face me.

"Hello, dear. How was your week?" She pushed up her glasses.

"Very good," I said, kissed her on her forehead and touched her feet.

She held my cheeks in her palms, stroked my near cheek.

I now stood facing her.

"Did you meet with the General again?"

I nodded.

"How did it go?" She gazed at me.

I recounted to her the essentials of my second meeting with the General: he wants to be friends with me; we discussed books; I was surprised to learn he liked to read; he wants me to give him books to read. . . .

"Thank God! See, I told you there is nothing to worry about. I have not stopped praying the whole week." She stared into space. "Come to think of it, it is strange . . ."

"What is?"

"Him wanting to be your friend, and his fancy for books . . . it is as if we are talking about a different General."

"Indeed. But, I can assure you that his intentions are true. He is going through a change of heart . . . a spiritual awakening . . . I sense that he is eager to reform his reputation . . ."

"God may have sent you to him . . . to help him save himself . . . all the evil things he has done . . . the corruption, jailing people on false charges . . . killing many of our brave people who dared to speak out against his evil deeds . . . maybe God is giving him a chance through you . . . a chance for him to repent."

"Maybe. And I assure you that I am not in danger with him."

"Oh, I know you are not. My milk sustained you. I would feel it in my heart if you were in danger . . ."

"I believe you."

"I would feel it in my bones . . . my spirit will be disturbed . . ." She stared into space. "I know you are brave, but

I was thinking . . . the General must have really impressed you for you to now be so sure of your safety with him," she now said.

"He impressed me, yes."

"What did he say, eh? What did he do?"

"The comments he made, his behavior, he is often deep in thought . . . Besides, I feel it that something is happening to him deep inside . . . And I am glad to discover that he is interested in books . . . I think I may be able to influence his thoughts."

"I will pray for him. God will enter his heart and give him the strength to change his ways."

"Please do."

"It is about time he mended his way."

"Indeed."

I stood lost in thought; Mama stared into space.

I now looked at Mama. "Where is Mika?"

"She is in the garden," she said.

"I will come spend time with you before I sleep." I kissed her on her forehead.

"Okay, dear." She gazed at me.

"I will be okay, Mama. Do not worry."

"Why is my son the Savior?"

"Maybe I am not," I said, smiling.

Silent, she continued to gaze at me. She sighed, pushed up her glasses, turned to face her sewing machine, hunched over it, her feet poised to press on its pedal.

I went to my study, tossed my bag on the bench chair and went into the kitchen, poured some cold pineapple juice into a big tumbler and headed for the backyard.

"Burẹ́wà."

"Angel! When did you arrive?" Mika smiled at me. She was kneeling on the ground tilling the soil, a wide-rimmed straw hat shielding her head from the fiery sun.

"Not long," I said and kissed her. "Here." I handed her the juice.

She drank it in rapid gulps.

"Thank you, dear. I needed that." She took off her hat

and wiped the sweat off her forehead with the back of her hand.

"You had a good week?"

"Yes, great, in fact. How long have you been out here?"

"Two hours. A bit longer, perhaps."

"That is enough. It is too hot."

"Just a little bit more cleaning of the bed. I need to get rid of the thorns. They are choking the vegetables."

"Let me help you some." I started to roll my shirtsleeve.

"No, no. I'm almost done. I don't trust you with my vegetables." She smiled.

I had once helped her and had left thorns that would have mushroomed and choked some vegetables if Mika had not timely noticed them.

"I did not study agriculture, you know."

"I didn't either." She stuck out her tongue at me.

I mimicked her.

"Well hurry up. I want to spend time with my woman. Besides, I want to tell you about my second meeting with the General."

"What second meeting? You met him again?"

"Last night. He sent his men to get me."

She gazed at me.

I feigned ignorance.

"Don't play with me. How did it go?"

"Fantastic. You would not believe it." I smiled.

"Give me a few minutes. I'm almost done."

"Okay."

. . .

Later, stretched out face up on the bench chair in my study, my head resting on a pillow propped on the arm-rest of the chair, the back of Mika's head resting on my heart, my arms wrapped round her ribcage, lightly touching her breasts, I recounted to her what had transpired on my second visit with the General.

"So, dear, I have a huge responsibility . . . which literature do you think I should give him? . . . In fact, he has made it easy to decide because he said that at this point in his life he is most interested in literature on metaphysics, philosophy, political theory and economic theory . . . and he wants to read African novels."

"African novels?"

"Yes. I convinced him to read them."

She stared into space, her heart beating a steady rhythm on my arm.

"You can't believe how excited I am. The General is a dormant intellectual! Wonders never cease to happen . . . humans, what a phenomenon, what a curious creature we are . . . Angel, do you know what this means? The heart of Gidaland is clutching at your feet to help him revive his intellectual pulse," she now said.

"Incredible, I know," I said.

The prime task in my family that weekend was deciding which literature to give the General. Mama volunteered to cook all the meals for the entire weekend. "My contribution to the General's salvation," she said, smiling. That gave Mika and me uninterrupted time to focus on discussing and listing the literature, and assembling the ones available at her library, and mine there in Freedom House. What a heady weekend it was. Seated on the floor in Mika's study, and later in mine, literature strewn about us as if we were graduate students at work on their dissertations, we debated, sometimes heatedly, the entries we made on the list. The only times we took leave of the task were when we went to the dining room to eat, or when physiology compelled it. Too excited to sleep properly we mostly napped. We did not love dance that weekend. That had never happened before.

By late Sunday night, we had agreed on a final list and had assembled the literature available at our libraries there in Freedom House.

Early Monday morning I left Freedom House and the tranquility of Boyo village for the bungalow and the hustle and bustle of the city.

On the night of the Thursday of that week, exactly a week after my second meeting with the General, Ibrahim and his men visited me. As usual, Ibrahim was cordial. "Good evening, sir. His Excellency sent me. His Excellency said you would understand, sir," he said. Mika had neatly packed in a carton the literature we had taken from our libraries in Freedom House, and I had taken the rest on the list from our libraries here in the bungalow and added them to those in the carton and taped it. There the carton was on the floor of my study waiting patiently to go fulfill its destiny. I dragged it to the living room, my back agonizing. Ibrahim looked at it, and then at me. "I will be back, sir," he said. He soon returned with one of his men, the one who usually sat beside the driver when they come to chauffeur me to the General's secret villa-den. And there they were, two tall and burly men. They bent down, grabbed the carton at its sides and, groaning, hoisted it.

"Good night, sir."

"Good night, Ibrahim," I said.

**Works Cited**

*Dangerous Love* by Ben Okri, London: Phoinix House 1996.

"Among the Silent Stones", "The Human Race is Not Yet Free", "Redeeming the World", and "While the World Sleeps" are from *A Way of Being Free* by Ben Okri, London: Phoinix House, 1997.

"An African Elegy", and "Lament of the Images" are from *An African Elergy* by Ben Okri, London: Vintage, 1997.

*The Soccer War* by Ryszard Kapuscinski, New York: First Vintage International Edition, 1992, published by Vintage Books, a division of Random House, Inc.

"Slave Song," lyrics by Sade Adu, Angel Music.

Grateful acknowledgement is made for the works cited; any omissions are regreted.